WHEN DARKNESS FINDS YOU

CHRIS COOPER

When Darkness Finds You

Published by Dreadful Media

Enjoy the book? Please consider leaving a review at goodreads.com or amazon.com. Every review helps. Receive free stories, news of new publications, and exclusive offers by signing up for our newsletter at WWW.DREADFULMEDIA.COM

SPECIAL THANKS

Sean Caballero
Dave Cutler
Sterling Finkbine
Morgan Leigh
Molly Snodgrass
Petra Gisela Sørensen
Rob Steinberger

CHAPTER ONE

The sound reminded me of a snore, a violent sucking in of air through his lungs then out through the gaps in his teeth, all in mechanical succession. Only he wasn't sleeping. He wasn't awake either. He wasn't much of anything anymore, just an empty vessel drifting out to sea after its captain had long ago gone overboard.

I held his limp hands and rubbed his bald head as his sporadic gray stubble scratched my palm. His wedding band slid clumsily on his skeletal ring finger as I laced my fingers through his. He'd worn that ring every day since Mom passed when I was twelve. I squeezed his hand. He used to squeeze back. Not anymore.

When he held his breath, I held mine, too, as I waited in agony for the next exhale. And just as my ears shut out everything but the man's breath, he took his last.

I heard his breathing every night in my dreams, even when I tried to dull my senses with a bottle of wine or a sleeping pill. The sound was impossible to ignore, like a ringing in the ears so intense that I could almost see it. I heard it even while standing over his coffin, the rhythmic rush of air, drowning out his colleague's eulogy. Dad didn't want a priest, a pastor, or anyone of the sort at his funeral. Even in death, the man had his way.

A gust of autumn air pulled me from my daze as it licked the back of my neck and blew my hair in front of my face. I swept it over my shoulders and looked down at his dark wooden coffin, suspended carefully over a modest hole in the earth, just large enough to fit it. We used to come to this cemetery to visit Mom and always walked the path of oak trees until we reached her headstone. "You'll come here to visit me one day," he'd said once, not realizing the cosmic weight that such a statement put on a teenager. I knew his words were true, but I hadn't expected the truth to arrive so soon.

His colleague stood stoic at the front of the coffin. "I am prepared to meet my Maker. Whether my Maker is prepared for the great ordeal of meeting me is another matter." He gave me a sympathetic smile. "If this quote hadn't been attributed to Winston Churchill, I would have sworn it came from Charlie."

After the eulogy, I stood at the side of his coffin as a hodgepodge of work buddies and acquaintances stopped to pay their respects. They muttered comforting phrases in my ears and patted me on the shoulder, but all I could concentrate on was a singular thought running through my mind. Eventually, I was the only one left at the gravesite, except for an impatient gravedigger perched on a bench underneath a large oak tree.

I brushed a tear from the corner of my eye and looked down into the black pit.

I'm alone.

It was a selfish thought, but I couldn't keep it from looping in my head.

I'm alone.

CHAPTER TWO

M y eyes traced the designs in the mismatched squares of examination room carpet. Whoever installed them hadn't bothered to line up the floral patterns, and the leaves clipped randomly into patches of cheap beige.

"At least I made it to fifty-five," he said.

"They said they could treat it." I sobbed. "Treatment could give you a few more years."

His eyebrows scrunched as he searched for a response. "It is what it is." His expression softened as if he was relieved the words made sense. That, coming from a man who'd spent most of his life studying the philosophical greats, could have been misconstrued as an oversimplified bit of wisdom. He couldn't find the words because the large black spot burrowing itself deep into the right side of his brain had wiped them from his repertoire.

Glioblastoma. The more I rolled the term around on my tongue, the more imaginary it sounded. I'd chalked up Dad's recent radio silence to the bouts of hibernation he was prone to on occasion. He lived in a two-bedroom by himself, on the other side of town, and would lock himself away in his study whenever he worked on a new book or article. "I couldn't be bothered with the real world, chickadee," he'd say when he finally reemerged.

Something had been different this time. The call from his editor tipped me off. Dad had submitted his monthly article to *Modern Verve*, the culture magazine he'd written for his entire career. His latest submission had been garbled nonsense. When I called to check on him, he managed little more than a hello. When I pushed him to speak, he sounded as if he'd made up his own language. I thought it was a stroke at first, but after I called 911 and Dad had a thorough evaluation, doctors discovered the large mass and bits of cancerous shrapnel lacing his brain.

How could I not have noticed earlier? I hated myself for it, for not calling more often or randomly stopping by and forcing my way into his hermitage. The guilt slithered between my ears as I lay awake at night.

I looked up once more from the floor, but Dad had vanished.

"Dad?" I called out. The room itself was only a few feet wide, and he had nowhere to hide. The mismatched carpet tiles swirled around me, and the room went dark.

I awoke in a pool of cold sweat and wiped away the rogue strands of black hair plastered to my forehead. I hadn't been much of a dreamer prior to Dad's death, but in the two months since, vivid dreams had become a part of my nightly routine. Some were mundane—Dad and I eating dinner together or going on a walk. I hated waking up from those. Others were much darker—sitting in waiting rooms and reliving Dad's chemo treatments. But eventually, Dad stopped making regular appearances—alive at least. My subconscious seemed to have come to grips with his death, and dinners became funerals and visits to the graveyard. I yearned for the old dreams, even the dark ones when his voice lingered in my ears, and for a moment upon waking, I would swear he was still alive. I missed him, and it was slowly settling in that he would never come back.

I wiped the crust from my eyes and stared at the chandelier of vampire bats suspended from the ceiling. I'd crafted the creatures from aluminum foil and latex. I pushed myself up against the headboard, and my eyes hit the black fleur-de-lis patterns painted on the eggplant-colored walls. Coffin-shaped bookshelves sat on either side of an antique writing desk, lined with everything from Gothic horror classics to a self-published book about a possessed refrigerator, a novel that I'd been sent to review on my vlog. Creatures leaned in from the wood cabinets next to me, my resin recreations of Frankenstein, Lon Chaney's Phantom, and other relics of the celluloid era.

Since Dad's death, waking up in that room had become claustrophobic, as if I started each day with someone adding to the weight already positioned directly above my heart. I made my living by peddling macabre wares and horror-inspired creations, but the constant reminders of death had become too over-whelming.

I flipped back the black comforter and slid my legs over the edge of the bed. I passed through the hallway past old horror movie posters and pulled back the heavy black curtains in the living room. Sunlight washed over the bleak interior, and I squinted until the scene below came into focus. The Sunday-morning crowd was milling around the square below, mean-dering between the coffee shop and the hodgepodge of indie storefronts lining the streets.

Renting an apartment in the historic district had always been a dream of mine. As soon as I'd made enough money to upgrade from my small studio in the bad part of town, I found a one-bedroom on the third floor of a hundred-year-old brick beauty, complete with glass doorknobs, crooked doorframes, and a few ghost stories of its own. The three flights of steps with no elevator was a drawback, but my feet had happily paid the price for more than a year.

I ignored the pile of dirty dishes in the sink—dishes that had been there so long I was hesitant to disturb them for fear of what I might find growing between the layers—and made my way to the coffee cupboard. My heart sank as a quick shake of the bag of beans resulted in an insufficient rattle. I eyed the half pot of cold coffee on the counter and grabbed the handle. An oily film had formed on the coffee's surface. "You haven't left the apartment for days. A little fresh air won't kill you," I said under my breath and dumped the cold sludge into the sink before desperation got the best of me. I grabbed my coat and a pair of sweatpants and pulled on a wool cap to cover the black rat's nest on top of my head.

Fall had quickly faded into winter. The long-dead leaves, once cheery shades of orange and yellow, had grayed and rotted. The trees in the park jutted from the earth like skeletal hands. I'd completely missed Halloween this year—and the small fortune that would have come with it. The town council had already tucked away the fall decorations and adorned the lampposts with cheery snowmen and Santa hats. The thought of Christmas made me sick to my stomach, and I swallowed hard to squelch the nausea.

A toy store had moved into the vacant storefront next to the coffee shop. I stood in front of the window and admired the intricately carved wooden robot standing next to an elaborate train set. That storefront would have been mine if I'd followed through with the grand plan that fell apart when Dad got sick.

I bought a chai latte at the coffee shop and sat for a few minutes, warming myself in the sun beaming through the front window. Then I took a lap around the shop to admire the new artwork. The artist had melted and warped vinyl records into abstract tribal masks. The shop owner kept a rotating exhibit of local art, and I knew most of the artists, although I didn't immediately recognize the new works.

"Lovely, aren't they?" The owner rounded the corner and cleared off the table next to me, her curly gray hair bobbing as she scrubbed a particularly dirty spot. "About time we get you in here again, Robin. Working on anything new?"

I forced a smile and buttoned my coat. "Taking a hiatus."

"I see." She doubled down on the spot. "Well, you know where to find me. I love your stuff. But don't wait too long for the muse to come knocking. Sometimes, you have to track it down."

Reminders of my artistic drought surrounded me: walls where my paintings used to hang, incomplete sculptures collecting dust in my apartment, and count-less emails asking me when my online shop would take orders again. Pain and tragedy were supposed to be artist fuel, but I was incapacitated by my own morbid success. I'd grown to hate my creations and wanted nothing more than to wipe them all away and start over. If I could, I would have locked myself in my bedroom and slept until my fans were long gone and I was a nobody again.

I should have turned left to head to my apartment, but something pulled me to the right instead. I passed the African clothing shop then the Mexican place and found myself in front of the small hardware store a few blocks down the street.

Today, I'm starting over.

CHAPTER THREE

The handle of the paint can dug into my fingers as I lugged the supplies up the steps to my apartment. I dropped my purchases next to the front door and, as I fished for the key in my peacoat pocket, stared down the imposing gargoyle knocker I'd hung last year.

My fascination with the macabre had started as a way of rebelling against a hyper-rationalist father who believed in neither the supernatural nor life after death. Even though the rebelliousness faded, my love of weird shit remained. The Snaps feed had started as a fluke. I'd posted a half dozen pictures of creepy figurines I'd sculpted then scenes of cosmic horror I'd sketched with charcoal. As I kept at it, my audience grew, and commission requests rolled in. An industrious college dropout—something else that must have left a knot in the pit of Dad's stomach—I created a small shop online and started taking orders. Between selling Ouija board pendants, creature sculptures, and Gothic paintings and pulling in a few brand deals here and there, I'd earned enough to cover my monthly rent, food, and art supplies. Eventually, I surpassed two hundred fifty thousand followers and even got one of those fancy *verified* symbols people seemed so fond of.

I stood in the doorway and stared into my grim life. The dark things I'd once loved had become unwelcome reminders that life was slowly but surely slipping away. Dad had died nearly two months ago, and ever since I'd started spending the night at my place again, I couldn't stand it. I needed to surround myself with life, to find in the waking world a reprieve from the shadows that shrouded my dreams.

When I reached my bedroom, I cleared my craft table. The marionette head of a hand-sculpted wolf boy looked up at me, and I slid him into a drawer to avoid his judgmental gaze. I pulled the table out from the wall and set the paint can on top of it. After taping off the baseboards of the room and lining the floor with plastic sheeting, I ran a roller of white paint across the purple walls. After the first coat, the purple still showed through in places, but I could already feel my spirits lifting.

By the time the orange glow of dusk slipped

through a crack in the curtains, I'd pulled the display cases of horror collectibles into the living room and coated the bedroom walls with two solid coats of paint. The bat chandelier lay in a tangled heap at the foot of my bed, and I'd switched the bedsheets from black to a cheery light blue.

I stepped back and admired the whitewashed bedroom. Although the rest of my apartment still looked like something out of a horror movie, the bedroom was extraordinarily bland. I lay on my bed, looked at the wonderfully boring white ceiling, and took a deep breath, letting the smell of fresh paint fill my nostrils. Maybe the physical labor had exhausted me, or perhaps I'd inhaled too many paint fumes, but for the first time in days, I fell into a deep sleep.

I awoke to a buzz from the nightstand. As I reached for my phone, my hand weaved between a half-filled glass of water and a stack of paperbacks. I'd slept for three hours solid, and notifications lined my phone screen. My gut churned with guilt. I'd gone AWOL since Dad died. Friends had tried to get in touch, but I couldn't bring myself to return their calls or texts. Every offer for help dredged up feelings I had been trying to keep at bay. And it was awful how people looked at me, their eyes wide with pity but their hearts secretly relieved that they weren't in my position.

I read the first text. *Where the fuck are you?*

Five missed calls preceded the line of expletive-laced messages.

Tyler had a foul mouth. I'd always liked that about him. He was an urban explorer I'd met at an influencer meetup a few years back, and I'd helped him launch an online magazine last year. The guy took stunning photos but couldn't lay out a spread to save his life. Tyler had reached out a few times to see how I was doing. I felt bad for not responding, but I'd been busy trying to sweep my life up off the floor.

I tapped the first voicemail message and held the phone to my ear.

"Robin. Jesus Christ. Owen's dead." Tyler's voice cracked. "I'm really sorry to break the news to you like this, but Amy just called. He killed himself, Robin. He posted the whole damn thing to their Snaps feed. He hung himself right in front of the fucking camera." He sniffled as he tried to compose himself. "Look, I was supposed to head up to Auburn to shoot some of their work in progress at the new house, so I thought I'd go anyway and see if she needs any help. I know you're probably going through hell right now, but you and Amy always got along, and she mentioned you when I called. If you've got shit to do with your family, I totally get it, but I wanted to put the offer out there. Meet up with me in Auburn. I'd like to see you, and I think Amy would too. She needs us."

I stared at my phone screen as if it were an alien creature spewing an unknown language. My eyes tingled in that pre-cry sort of way, only I had no more tears left to shed. That had to have been a joke.

I opened my Snaps app. A few thousand likes had trickled in, and my in-box was filled with a dozen direct messages, most of which were probably scams or dick pics. I tapped the search box and typed in the name of Amy and Owen's joint account.

This user cannot be found.

I typed Owen's name into my search engine and read the top search results—Influential Snaps User Livestreams Suicide.

"Shit," I said under my breath. My finger hovered over the link, but instead, I flipped my phone onto the comforter and lay in the dark. "I can't go through this again."

Amy and I had worked on a few projects together. She was a baker and crafter extraordinaire, and her husband was—had been—a carpenter. They both had a love for the paranormal, and it turned out there was a small market for haunted homes. Not only had they made a killing flipping historic houses with dark histories, but they'd garnered an online following too. They started their feed shortly after mine, and last year, they'd bought a house in New York to flip for the camera and turn into their dream home. *But they were happy.* Owen always had a smile on his face, and their careers were taking off. *How could he have killed himself?*

I took a deep breath, and my exhale filled the room. "I need to go. I have to go." I waited for the dark to tell me I'd been through enough and that I should continue my self-imposed exile. But the void provided no comfort. It never had. I counted down as if I were a rocket ship preparing for blastoff. And when I reached zero, I pushed off the bed and into the abyss.

CHAPTER FOUR

I ran my fingers along a row of books lining Dad's study shelf. He kept his favorites within reach of his office chair. Plato, Mill, Aristotle. The names all meant something profound to the man. I could see him at his desk, thumbing through the pages and dragging his fingers along the rows of black ink, searching for a fleeting bit of wisdom needed to tie an article together.

Jason, Dad's longtime scotch buddy, financial advisor, and will executor, leaned against the edge of Dad's cherry desk and pulled a small steno pad from the pocket of his plaid suit jacket. "You sure you want to donate all these?"

"No," I replied, "but I don't have room for any of this stuff at my place."

"You could always put his books in storage. You'll have plenty to cover it, and I could set up the move for you. Hell, by the time I've sorted his finances, you could probably buy a house for yourself and another just to store his books." He straightened his silver bifocals and scribbled a few notes.

"I'd just be prolonging the inevitable. I'll never read any of these. No sense in saving them when they could go to someone who might actually enjoy them." Dad had tried to foster a love of the philosophical greats, but I could never love them like Dad had. Those books were his babies, not mine.

Jason pointed at the top shelf, where Dad had kept a respectable row of first editions. "At least let me have those appraised."

I scanned the shelf, and my eyes caught an over-ripened-avocado-colored spine sticking out over the edge. I slid the wooden step stool across the hardwood floor, climbed on top, and pulled the book loose from the shelf. On the cover, an eagle gripped a gnome in its beak and carried it over a city skyline. Gold letters spelled out *Grimm's Fairy Tales* across the front, and snow accumulated on the top of each letter. I stepped down from the stool and ran my hand over the aged cover.

Typing *grief* into a search engine would spew out countless clickbait articles and top-ten lists, but I had found a quote that described my psyche since Dad's death. Unfortunately, I had closed the browser tab without saving it, but it went something like this: "Grief is like an ocean. Sometimes the seas are calm, and sometimes the waves crash against the sides of the boat in unrelenting fury."

The wave started as a tingling sensation in my stomach and rose up through my throat until it left my mouth in a poorly hidden cry. I kept my back toward Jason but was certain he'd heard me.

He awkwardly fished for the phone in his pocket. "I've got to make a quick call. I'll give you a minute."

"I'm fine," I replied, but he'd already left the room. I tucked the book under my arm and returned to the living room. A baby monitor sat on the end table next to Dad's gaudy seventies-era couch. I'd kept the other monitor on his bedside table so I could hear him from the living room. I'd slept on the couch while he was sick. He had a second bedroom but had converted it into his study, lining the walls with books and leaving no room for another bed in his tiny apartment. The man had money, and I couldn't figure out why he had sardined himself into this tiny place—at least, tiny for the stacks of books he'd crammed inside. Considering how large the man had lived, his life had ended so small.

An ugly autumn-leaves pattern covered the couch, and it was as comfortable as a burlap sack. I'd have paid someone to take it out back and axe it to death. I plopped down onto one of the flat cushions, and my eyes darted to his closed bedroom door. I hadn't been inside since his death. I'd called the home health nurse after he passed, and she'd come to take his final vitals. She contacted the funeral home for me, and they sent two people to collect the body. One was nice enough, but the other was a pale shrimp of a kid who had as much tact as the sofa on which I sat.

"Where is he?" he'd asked.

I pointed at the closed bedroom door, and I would have sworn the twerp rolled his eyes.

"Oh, I'm sorry. Am I inconveniencing you? Would you like me to drag him out here to make it easier on you? I don't think he'll be able to walk by himself."

I later asked the funeral home director about the two boys. "Just interns from the local school," he'd replied. "I don't do heavy lifting anymore because of my back. I leave that for the young 'uns."

I felt relieved when Dad died, although I wouldn't have admitted that if asked. Watching him struggle to say basic sentences devolved into fishing fingers full of food out of his mouth when he forgot how to chew. He still managed the occasional "I love yous," but even those were few and far between. Reading was a no go, so the nurse and I set his TV up in his bedroom and traded in his old wooden bed frame for a hospital bed.

"As long as I have my mind and my daughter," he

would say, "I'll be happy to live to one hundred." He lost his mind, and by the end, I wasn't sure he knew he had a daughter.

"You look like shit." Jason returned from the kitchen and pulled me from my daydream.

I admired the man's honesty and cracked a smile. "You know how to make a girl feel good about herself."

He sat next to me on the old couch. "Sometimes, it's better to hear the truth. Are you getting enough sleep?"

"Every night brings an existential nightmare."

Jason's eyes widened.

"I'm just kidding." I was only slightly kidding. People didn't want the truth. Some could take a watered-down version, but most just wanted to hear that you were "fine" or "doing better." It was tiring. No one wanted to hear that I felt as if the seams holding the fabric of my life together were fraying, and as the patchwork pieces broke apart, all I saw was chaos underneath. It was all chaos. Emptiness.

But the lie had worked, and his expression softened. "Where did you say you were headed?"

I pulled out my phone to check the time. "I'm driving up to Auburn to see a friend. Her husband just died."

"Damn," he replied. "When it rains, it pours. What happened?"

"He killed himself." This was the first time I'd mentioned Owen's death out loud, and I was surprised by how cold I sounded as the words left my lips.

Jason looked as if I'd just punched him in the gut. "Jesus. Are you all right? I mean, you've been through enough already."

His look made me uncomfortable, like he was expecting some kind of sorrowful performance. I grabbed the book and stood before his stare became unbearable. "I gotta get going. Promised I'd get to Auburn by one."

"Sure. I don't want to keep you." He walked me to the door. "We should be able to wrap up the estate soon. I'll have a few things for you to sign, but it can wait for now. Looks like your dad had most of his accounts in order and listed you as the beneficiary, so we'll be able to get everything into your name pretty quickly. And I'm going to look through those books before I donate anything. Trust me. You'll thank me later."

As I went to leave, he grabbed my hand. "I know the last thing you need right now is advice, but when my parents died years ago—"

I pulled away. "You're right. Advice is the last thing I need right now."

"Oh." Jason shrank back into the apartment.

I massaged my temples hard with my thumb and middle fingers. "I'm sorry. I didn't mean—"

Jason shrugged. "You don't owe me an explanation. Everyone deals with grief differently. Be easy on yourself."

"Thanks," I replied. "I appreciate all your help. I wouldn't know what to do without you."

"No problem. You can thank me by taking care of yourself."

"I'll do my best."

As I left Dad's complex, the buzz of a fleet of leaf blowers greeted me. One of the gardeners stopped long enough for me to pass, and I gave him a weak wave as I reached for my car door. Once inside, I slunk down in my seat to avoid making a scene and cradled the book in my lap. I flipped through the pages, and the ink sketches brought back memories of bedtime stories and countless tuck-ins. I held it in front of me to avoid getting the pages wet.

My phone rattled against the gearshift, and I shut the book and placed it gingerly onto the passenger seat. I wiped the tears from the corners of my eyes then read the message from Tyler.

Just about to take off from Detroit. Should be to Amy's within the next few hours, once I land and load all my stuff into the rental. Excited to see your face!

A thumbs-up emoji was all I could muster in reply.

I would stay at Amy's for a few days for Owen's funeral then return and put my life back in order. If I didn't reopen the online shop or start posting to Snaps soon, I'd start hemorrhaging followers and would have to flip burgers to pay rent. Except for the inheritance... Jason had hinted at it, and although I'd seen a few of Dad's bank statements, I had no clue how much money he had squirreled away. Money couldn't bring Dad back, but it could buy me a little time.

CHAPTER FIVE

The Auburn streets were lined with pristine painted ladies and Colonial Revival homes that eyed passersby with regal gazes. As I drove farther into the city, though, elegant mansions became run-down Craftsmen, and lush parks and green spaces became gas stations and fast-food joints. Litter skittered along the cracked asphalt roads, and the town's layout shrunk in on itself as houses sat closer together.

I first glimpsed Amy's place as I drove along the overgrown hedgerows bordering the property. A castle-like turret jutted out above the crest of a slate roof. The land must have been a quarter acre and sat in odd contrast to the small neighborhood plots surrounding it.

Amy's gate hung open, and one of the heavy iron panels had been removed from its hinges and lay crooked against the fence. As I pulled onto the gravel drive, I noticed large spiraling *Es* sculpted and affixed to each of the gate panels.

The brick house was three stories tall, and its walls were speckled with single-pane windows of various shapes and sizes. A porch wrapped around the left side of the building, leading to a painted rotunda roof at its center. Olive-colored trim and ornate filigree laced the building and hinted at its once extravagant aesthetic, and my eyes hopped from turret to window to fancy spindle. The brick walls of the Victorian varied in color in places, probably from repairs over the years.

In a previous life, I would have been ecstatic to visit any home with a ghost story, let alone a creepy masterpiece like the house that sat in front of me. But all ghost stories came with a price, real-life death and grief, which I hadn't realized until I'd paid the price myself. I imagined my dad stuck between two worlds, trying to take care of unfinished business as a spectral wayward wanderer. The thought made me sick to my stomach.

I knew little of the spook that had brought Amy and Owen to this crumbling estate, but whatever force lived here had just gained a ghostly friend in Owen. I knew what it was like to lose a father, but I couldn't imagine losing a partner.

I yanked my bag from the passenger seat floorboard

and approached the front entrance. The staircase started narrow at the top then spilled outward onto the walkway, accented by a curved handrail. I climbed the steps and searched for the doorbell next to the paneled double doors. Although brass doorknobs protruded from each, a third spindly knob stuck out from chest height on the right. I reached for it and twisted, and a tepid ring gurgled from inside.

Amy opened the door. Her jet-black bangs hung over her forehead, forming a perfect line across it, and her shoulder-length locks were straight and shiny. Spiraling tattoos poked out from the collar of her T-shirt. She was so small beneath the high ceilings, and the ornate woodwork surrounding her seemed to over-power her shrunken frame. "Hi." She gave a meek wave.

I leaned in and squeezed her tight. "I'm so sorry."

"Me too," she replied. "Can't imagine what you're going through, with your dad and all. How are you doing?"

"I'm okay." Tears welled in the corners of my eyes. I thought back to my time in Dad's apartment after his death. "How can you stand to be in this house right now?"

She sniffled. "Not much of a choice. Our lease at the apartment ended, so I either had to move in or find somewhere else to live. Seemed dumb not to move in, considering we've got eager fans waiting for house updates." She pulled away.

"You just moved in? I thought you and Owen were already living here together?"

She glanced at her watch, and her expression shifted as if an internal switch had been flipped. "I've got to check the cookies. Want to come help me?"

"Uh, sure."

She turned her back to me. "Great! Then I can show you your room," she added as her voice trailed down the hall.

I followed Amy into the kitchen. Water damage had stained the ceiling above the foyer, and the plaster was crumbling in places. The hallway wallpaper had been stripped, revealing large cracks in the wall underneath. As we reached the end of the hall, I peered into the living room on the other side. Plastic sheeting lined one window and pulsed from the breeze outside. The single-pane glass had been removed, probably broken ages ago, and boards lined the frame. Blankets lay on a black leather sofa perched in front of an entertainment center and large flat-screen TV. The baseboards and crown molding had been taped off with blue painter's tape, although nothing in the room had yet been painted. Several repairs had been made to the plaster walls and crown molding, leaving ugly white splotches of Spackle in the even uglier dingy yellow paint. I was over-whelmed for her.

"Come help me," she said over my shoulder.

"Sorry." I twisted around to face the kitchen.

Her kitchen had been completely renovated. Black cabinetry lined its walls, accented by brushed gold handles and fixtures. A chandelier hung over the kitchen island, where Amy stood examining a tray of sugar cookies resting on the white marble countertop.

She twisted one of the gas knobs on the six burner-stove.

"Amy, your kitchen. It's—"

"Stunning," she replied. "Thanks. After Owen patched the roof and had all the vitals taken care of, he wanted to make sure I had a kitchen for the feed. It's something, isn't it?"

Why did he do it? The question hit me, but I swallowed the impulse to ask. Owen and Amy had seemed to have so much going for them, and I couldn't imagine what could have driven the man to kill himself.

"Once the cookies cool, I'll decorate them then do a shoot for the feed," she said.

"The feed?"

She smiled. "They're letting me have it back. Followers and all. It's got to go through one final round of approval, but I should be able to post again by tonight."

"That's fast." Considering the circumstances, I couldn't understand why she was so eager to get back to work.

"What do you mean?" Her tweezed black brows furrowed.

My fingers traced the indent of the phone against my jeans. "Nothing. I'm sorry. I didn't mean anything by it. It's just—I don't know how you do it. I haven't posted anything for two months now. I just can't bring myself to do it. The store's still down too. How can you even think about the Snaps right now?"

Amy locked eyes with me and scowled. "It's all I have. I've built my entire career on this shit—the baking, the houses. With Owen gone, I have no clue how I'm going to flip more houses or how I'm even going to fix this one. I'm screwed." She gripped the edges of the counter and leaned in. "So while I try to figure out how the hell I'm going to salvage any of this, I'm going to bake some fucking cookies and try to win back the people who just watched my husband hang himself on livestream." She looked at me as if I'd killed Owen myself, and for a moment, I wanted to run screaming from the room. Then I remembered how I'd snapped at people after Dad died, how I pretended everything was fine and pounced on anyone who dared suggest otherwise. "I'm sorry. I didn't mean to upset you. I'm happy to help."

Her eyes went red and glossy as I reached for her hand across the counter. When our hands touched, she abruptly pulled hers away. "I'm sorry." A look of panic crossed her face. "I'm sorry," she panted. "I just don't know what I'm going to do."

I wiped my eyes and rounded the corner of the island. "It's okay. You don't have to figure it all out today. Take a minute and breathe." I wasn't sure whether I'd meant the advice for her or myself.

She suddenly sobbed, and I ran my hand up and down her back.

The groaning of the doorbell carried through the hallway and into the kitchen.

Amy grabbed the towel from the handle of the oven door and blotted her eyes. "Must be Tyler. Please, don't tell him about this. I just haven't processed. I'll be fine."

She stepped toward the hallway, but I grabbed her by the arm. "Are you sure you want us to stay? After Dad... I just wanted to be alone. It won't hurt my feelings if you need time to yourself. I'm sure Tyler would understand. We could find a hotel nearby or something."

"No, I want you here," she replied. "I don't know what I would do if I was in this house by myself." She took off for the front door, and I followed close behind.

Tyler stood on the porch with a backpack slung

over his shoulder and a duffel bag in hand. The breeze blew his curly brown hair, and he tried to use his fingers as an impromptu comb. He wore a gray-and-black striped shirt under a black bomber jacket. "Jesus fucking Christ, Amy. I'm so sorry." He leaned in and hugged her with his free hand. "Owen was one hell of a guy. How are you holding up?" He sighed. "What a stupid fucking question. I'm sorry—I just don't know what to say. This is all so shitty."

Amy smiled. "It's okay. I'm glad you came."

"Of course," he replied. "I've got the rest of the gear in the rental van, but are you sure you still want to shoot? I figure it's probably the last thing you want—"

"I'll be fine. The show must go on."

Tyler's mouth hung open as if prepared to speak.

I tugged on his jacket sleeve. "It's good to see you."

He dropped his bag on the ground and rested his chin on my head as he wrapped his spindly arms around me. "Good to see you too. Sorry to hear about your dad. You guys have the shittiest fucking luck."

"Thanks." I buried my head in his jacket. As he pulled away, his hand lingered on the small of my back. It was a hint, but whether it was intentional or not, I couldn't be sure. Tyler might not have had the best vocabulary, but he was a good guy. Had things not gone south with Dad, I could have seen myself getting more involved with his magazine in Detroit and maybe even doing some artwork for his videos. The guy was building his own urban-exploring empire. I appreciated him keeping our nonbusiness affairs to himself. Most guys would brag about something like that but not Tyler.

Amy turned toward the staircase. "Let me show you guys to your bedrooms."

Tyler looked around the foyer. "This place is epic. I brought the new drone to get some exterior shots. Can't wait to try it out."

I grabbed my bag, and we followed Amy up the stairs to the second-floor hallway. The carpet had been ripped up and rolled to the end of the hall, revealing the warped, water-stained hardwood underneath.

I counted the doors along the hall. "How many bedrooms does this place have?"

"It's funny," she replied. "When we bought the place, the Realtor's info was all wrong. The database said the house had six bedrooms. We counted five. It's over four thousand square feet, easily." She twisted the glass knob to one bedroom at the end of the hall. "Owen wasn't able to finish all the bedrooms before... Things are still a mess. Sorry."

The room was an odd mix of antique and IKEA. The same dated floral wallpaper from the hallway lined the walls. A Singer sewing machine stand had been pushed up against the wall next to a scratched-up cherry wardrobe. A modern queen-sized bed sat against the wall with a pair of gunmetal lamps perched on nightstands on either side. A gaudy gold oval mirror hung against the far wall, its surface splotchy and permanently clouded with age.

"It's not much," she said, "and the only other bedroom that's in decent shape has a huge crack in the window. I've got extra blankets, but whoever takes that one better like the cold."

"I don't mind," Tyler replied. "Robin can have this one."

"You sure?" I asked.

Tyler grinned. "I spent Saturday in an old movie theater underneath a dead shopping mall. It had filled with water and frozen over like a gross skating rink. I can handle a draft."

"Fair enough," I replied.

Amy pointed down the hall. "In that case, Tyler, your bedroom is back toward mine."

"Where's your bedroom?" I asked.

"I'm just on the other side of the landing in the master. It's the room with the balcony off the second floor." She turned toward me. "Make yourself at home. I'll show Tyler to his room, then we can finish the cookies, take a few pics, and I'll order dinner."

"Sounds good." I tossed my bag onto the bed and crossed the room to the far window. The room was chilly but not unbearable, and the single-pane glass was cold to the touch. I could only imagine how cold Tyler's room must be.

The window looked out on the side yard and the street beyond the iron fence. I was surprised that Amy had been willing to buy a place in such an obviously bad part of town. *Even if she fixes it up, who would even want to buy it? And how the hell is she going to do all this work by herself?*

Landscaping must have been the lowest item on the priority list given the winter weather. A small pergola sat sad and slumping against the house. Slimy algae coated the rotting beams, some of which had collapsed. Patches of dead rose brambles had been pulled from the fence and thrown into a heap next to a large mound of topsoil. *That must be where they found the body.*

CHAPTER SIX

I slid the tall pocket door aside and stuck my head into the parlor. The room still smelled of wood stain and paint. A fireplace sat on the far wall. Its mantel consisted of hand-carved vines that ran up from the tiled hearth as their branches laced together, dotted occasionally by delicate mahogany leaves. Stained glass windows sat on either side of the fireplace and cast a green glow on the refinished hardwood. The wainscoting had been stripped of its chipped, yellowed paint and sanded and stained to match the fireplace. The room had been completely refinished.

"Hey," Tyler whispered from behind.

Terrified, I squealed. "You scared the crap out of me."

He held his index finger to his lips.

"What?" I whispered, although there was little

point considering the sound I had just made. Surely the entire house had heard.

He edged to the entrance of the room and cautiously peeked inside. His mouth contorted at an odd angle. "Keep this door closed."

"Why? This room is beautiful."

"This is *the* room."

"The room? What do you mean?"

"The room where Owen hanged himself," he whispered.

My heart dropped. "Oh God. How do you know?"

"Everything all right out there?" Amy's voice carried down the hallway from the kitchen.

I immediately slid the door closed behind me and pushed past him. "Thanks for the warning," I whispered as Amy rounded the corner.

Amy had put in extensions and teased her hair into a tall beehive. She wore a tight apron with a Black Widow hourglass adorning the front.

"Everything's fine." I braced myself against the doorframe. "He just snuck up on me is all."

"Would you guys give me a hand? I'm ready to shoot." She didn't wait for a reply and turned toward the kitchen. She sat in front of the bright LED makeup mirror on the kitchen island and ran a thick slash of eyeliner across her lid. "Tyler, you can set up the lights, and Robin, you're going to be my kraken."

"Kraken?" I'd heard of the giant cephalopod before but bore no resemblance.

She waved me over to the counter and lifted a long papier-mâché tentacle from behind the island. "I'm going to attach the cookie tray to the top of this, and you'll hold it up from behind the counter."

Tyler chuckled. "That thing looks like it's about to break in half. Do you want me to try to reinforce—"

Amy shot him a spiteful glance. "It'll look fine once we set up the shot," she snapped. "Just fix the lights and hold the commentary."

Tyler shrugged. "Suit yourself." He slid the tabletop LED panels in front of her and positioned them until the lighting was just right.

I knew exactly how she felt. In the first few days after Dad's death, I'd packed every spare moment with work and tried to fill orders that were already behind. Amy was knee-deep in denial and headed straight toward anger and overwhelm. But it wasn't our job to push her there before she was ready. I knew it wouldn't take much—a burned batch of cookies or a minor setback of some sort. I had thrown a plaster mold across the room after it failed to set correctly and was still picking bits of the stuff out of my apartment rug weeks later. "Those cookies look amazing." I straightened the legs of Amy's tripod and framed her in the center of the camera's viewfinder.

She arranged the iced bat cookies on the tray then pressed an adhesive pad to the bottom and mounted the tray to the top of the octopus tentacle.

"Thanks, doll. Just watch out. This thing *is* a little flimsy." She handed me the bare PVC pipe that protruded from the bottom. "Owen was always better at making props. I want you to crouch behind the island and hold this up next to me." She pointed at one of the light stands on the counter. "That's too far away, Tyler. Move it closer and to the left."

I could sense Tyler's impending eye roll, but he swallowed hard and did as told. The guy had done his own lighting for years. If anyone but Amy had made the comment, he would have pushed back.

I stooped behind the island and held the tentacle up with Amy's guidance.

"That's good. Hold it right there." She shifted with each shutter snap, striking slightly different poses, none of which I could see from underneath her.

Tyler pulled the camera from the tripod and rounded the counter.

Amy looked into the viewfinder and flipped through the raw shots. "This one will work. Just need to do a little touch-up."

My hand cramped as I steadied my grip on the bare pipe. "Can I put this down now?"

"Oh, sorry." Amy popped the serving tray off the end of the tentacle.

I set the appendage on the counter and leaned in next to Amy to see the shot. She'd pressed her cleavage against the edge of the counter as the mystery tentacle lifted the platter to her side. The girl knew what she was doing. Anyone who had swiped through her feed would have found dozens of shots like that—creep combined with just the right amount of sex. It would get a lot of likes. I wasn't that savvy and didn't have the right assets to pull off that sort of look.

"Looks good," I said.

Tyler grinned. "You sure know how to work a tentacle."

I rolled my eyes. "You wish."

Tyler grabbed a cookie from the tray and bit the bat in half. A few moments later, he spit the chewed-up cookie into his hand. "God, what the hell did you put in these?"

Amy giggled. "The icing looked a little dry, so I brushed them with olive oil so they'd shine on camera."

"Instant karma," I added.

* * *

LATER THAT EVENING, we sat around the kitchen island as Tyler unzipped his backpack. "I think we can all agree life has been complete shit lately."

"Thanks for the reminder," Amy replied.

Tyler waved his hand dismissively then reached into his bag. "I thought you girls deserved a drink or twelve, so I picked up something special." He slid a wine-shaped bottle from inside, and I immediately recognized the stag logo.

"Velvet Antler," I said. "It was Dad's favorite bourbon."

Tyler tipped the end of the bottle in my direction. "All the more reason to have a taste."

"That stuff's two hundred bucks a bottle, and they only sell it by lottery," I replied. I flashed back to Dad's apartment. After weeks of lying in bed, the man's muscles had completely atrophied, and despite my and the nurse's best efforts to move him during the day, he wore the constant back pain on his face like his patchy gray beard. One evening, just past midnight, I heard some shuffling through the baby monitor. Something about the drone of the TV seemed to help him sleep, but he'd set himself up in bed and was looking at the TV screen with a vacant stare and slight grimace.

"Everything all right?" I asked, knowing good and well he couldn't answer.

His gaze shifted from the TV until it met mine. His

eyes grew wide and wild. He had a habit of looking through me, surely a symptom of his failing brain, but something in him seemed to have woken up. His eyes followed mine, and even though the connections between his brain and much of the rest of his body had been broken, I could tell he knew what was happening. He knew he was going to die, and for the first time since his diagnosis, he looked terrified.

I walked toward the side of his bed and reached for his hand as his eyes followed me across the room. "I love you, Dad."

He opened his mouth as if trying to speak.

"I'll be right back," I said.

I slipped into his office and reached for the bourbon bottle on a small serving cart next to the door. I held the bottle up to the light from the hallway. The man deserved the two fingers full left at the bottom. I grabbed a whiskey glass from the cart, emptied the bottle, and returned to his room. I knew I shouldn't have done it. The nurse would have been furious, but what was the worst that could happen?

He stared at me as I leaned in and held the glass to his nose. "Remember this?"

His arm shook as he reached and gripped the tumbler in his trembling fingers. He brought the glass to his lips as I guided his hand from underneath.

After he took a slow sip, I set the glass on the table,

and his eyes floated toward mine. The corner of one side of his mouth curled as if he were trying to smile, then his eyes returned to the TV, and he was gone once more.

"Still with us?" Tyler held a glass out in front of me.

"Yeah, sorry. What are we drinking to?"

Amy tipped her glass back and consumed its entire contents in a single gulp then gritted her teeth. "Burns a little."

Tyler's mouth hung open. "You're supposed to sip it, you fucking savage."

She tipped the glass again and captured the few drops that clung to the bottom. "You've got fancy tastes for a guy who crawls through sewers for a living."

He grinned. "It pays the bills."

I put my glass to my lips and sipped. I could play along, but the fancy bourbon was wasted on me too. Tyler could have filled the bottle with the cheap stuff from the local gas station, and I wouldn't have known the difference. It burned, tasted like death, and made my mind fuzzy in an anything's-possible kind of way.

He pointed at me. "Like that. Sip it."

Amy slid her glass across the table. "Hit me again, bartender."

He glared at her as he tipped the bottle and filled

her glass for a second time. "Sip it," he reiterated as he slid the glass across the counter.

Amy lifted the glass, stuck her pinky out, then gingerly tilted it. "So, do you all want to hear about the Lady in White?"

I knew that Amy and Owen had found human remains on the property but hadn't heard the details.

Tyler poured another bourbon. "That's your resident ghost, right?"

Amy nodded. "She's haunted this place for more than a century, apparently. Can't say she's made any appearances, though, at least not since Owen found those bones in the backyard."

Tyler's eyes widened. "So that was real? I figured you guys faked it for Snaps."

"Owen found them while digging up rosebushes out back. Called the cops and everything."

I leaned in. "Do you think it was her—the lady, I mean?"

"The bones were female and had definitely been there a while."

"Then what was her unfinished business?" Tyler asked.

"Someone bashed her skull in. Her body had never been properly laid to rest." Amy took another swig from her glass and shivered from the burn.

"Find any more information about her?" I asked.

"Been a little preoccupied." Amy scowled as if the events of the last few days had come rushing back.

"What did they do with the body?" Tyler was oblivious to the situation.

"Believe it or not, they identified her and found a next of kin. Last Owen checked, the police had released her remains."

"What a terrible way to go," Tyler added. "So you've never seen anything, you know, odd around here?"

Amy shook her head and looked down at the counter. "Not a thing."

Within the hour, we polished off the bottle of fancy bourbon then switched to the cheaper stuff. Amy ordered a couple of pizzas, and we sat around the kitchen island and swapped stories. I'd forgotten what drunken nights with friends were like, and for a few moments, I felt as if everything had gone back to normal.

CHAPTER SEVEN

I awoke from a bourbon-induced dream to the sound of Amy's voice slipping under the doorway. I couldn't remember how deep we'd made it into the second bottle, but my headache suggested we'd finished it. A cold draft hit me as soon as I threw the covers off, and I braced from the chill as I tiptoed down the hall, past Tyler's room and toward the staircase.

Amy sounded as if she were practicing a speech. Once I reached the doorway to the kitchen, I poked my head around the corner. She was putting finishing touches on her makeup as she talked to herself in the mirror. She gave her face one final inspection then pulled down her left eyelid and ran the tip of her index finger across it. She stared unblinking at the mirror as a teardrop formed and dripped down her cheek, bringing with it a tiny stream of mascara. She repeated the process with her right eye then examined her face once more before reaching for her cell phone. Amy took a deep breath then held the phone in front of her and tapped the screen.

"Good morning, guys. I don't really know how to start this video, so here goes." She sniffled. "Most of you know that Owen passed away a few days ago. Hell, most of you saw it. First, I want to apologize to anyone who saw the video before Snaps removed it and thank you all for your kindness through this incredibly tough time. I truly appreciate you and the support of the people at Snaps, who acted quickly and have been so understanding as I try to pull everything back together. I know Owen would have wanted me to see the new house project through to the end, and that's exactly what I plan to do. And last but not least, if you or someone you know suffers from depression, please know that you are not alone, but suicide is not the answer. If you or a loved one needs help, please swipe up to visit the National Suicide Prevention Association website." She tapped the screen again then set her phone on the counter. "Thank God that's over." She grabbed a tissue and blotted her tears.

I stepped backward toward the hallway but hit a creaking floorboard along the way.

Amy's head snapped toward me, and I tried to pass it off with a yawn as I entered the kitchen. "Morning."

"Morning," Amy replied.

I rounded the island and sat on a stool across from her. "You look like you've been crying. Everything okay?"

She looked down at the counter. "Just finished recording a new Snaps video. It'll be the first one since Owen."

"I'm sure your followers will come back in no time." The words felt odd on my tongue. I wanted to be supportive, but her fake crying left an uneasy knot in the pit of my stomach. I wasn't the best at dealing with grief, but I'd never seen someone fake it before, especially for a million strangers.

Amy grinned. "You'd think people would have dropped me when they saw the video, but I've gained fifty thousand since then. I guess people saw the story on the news."

The thought of people tuning in to view a personal tragedy made my stomach queasy, but for some reason, Amy was energized by it. I shook the thought from my mind and tried to change the subject. "Need help with anything this morning?"

"Nope, think I got it, but Tyler's outside with the drone. Why don't you go help him? He's getting some footage for my house-tour video." She examined her makeup in the mirror and dabbed her cheeks once more with a tissue.

I grabbed my coat from the hook by the door and wrapped my hand-knit orange scarf around my neck as I left the house.

Tyler straddled a black plastic chest in the front yard and lifted a heavy white contraption from inside of it.

"Wow." I moved in to inspect. "This must be the new toy you were talking about."

"You're a fucking genius." He set the drone gingerly on the ground. "You ever fly one of these things before?"

I looked down at the complex piece of machinery. The drone was shaped like a large X, with four propellers and a camera mount underneath. The bright-white finish and colored stripes reminded me of a bowling pin. "No. Is that an offer?"

"You wish. Unless you've got two grand laying around you're willing to spare if you run it into the side of the house."

"You mean for two grand, that thing can't steer itself?"

He scoffed. "Can't steer itself? This model can avoid objects from twenty feet out. It's probably harder to crash than it is to fly." He flipped a switch on the top of its chassis.

"Then what are you afraid of? Why can't I fly it?" I goaded.

"Because it's mine, and I want to fly it first." He pouted. "But you can watch." He pulled out his cell phone and slid it into an odd-looking controller. "See." He held the screen close enough for me to see. My sneakers were in the frame, as well as the front steps of the house. "I fly it through the app, and the camera feed streams directly to my phone."

"It takes pretty good video, then?"

"Pretty good video? It shoots in 4K at sixty frames per second."

Clueless, I stared at him with my mouth ajar.

"That means it shoots pretty good video." He pressed a button on the control pad. The drone propellers spun into a beehive-like buzz as the drone left the ground. For a moment, it hovered in place then twisted around at eye height to face us.

Tyler gestured for me to come closer and held out the screen. It showed us center frame, and I waved like a dork, not sure what else to do.

"I was just giving you a hard time. I'll let you fly it."

I pulled back. "After all that crap about running it into the side of the house."

Tyler grinned. "I'll be right here if you run into any problems."

He rested his hand on my back and peered over my shoulder as I took the controller.

I carefully pressed the left and right sticks, and the

drone twisted toward the house and gained altitude, drawing closer to the front of the house as it climbed. "It's nice of you to use the inaugural flight to help Amy with her house tour."

"Yeah," he replied, not breaking eye contact with the screen. "It's good practice. Some shoots I'm planning are in pretty tight spaces, and I want to make sure I can fly the damned thing before I send it through a tunnel."

"If I ask you something, will you promise not to bring it up to Amy?"

His eyes flashed toward mine then back to the screen. "Sure. What's up?"

"Has Amy been acting weird to you? I get Owen just died, and I'm not in a place to tell other people how to act, since I've been off the grid for weeks, but..."

"Weird how?"

"She was in the kitchen recording a video when I came downstairs. It looked like she was making herself cry. And whenever we talk about Owen, she dodges or talks about how much work she has to do on the house. But she never says anything about him. I don't get how she's so worried about her feed when her partner just died."

"The girl's probably wrecked," he replied. "Maybe she doesn't want to talk about him. And without an audience, she's nothing, especially if

Owen won't be around to help her flip any more houses."

His words felt like a punch in the gut. "You really think she's nothing without some stupid social network?"

"I'm sorry." He leaned in. "I didn't mean it that way. She's not nothing—you're not nothing. I just meant she might have gotten this house for a steal, but it'll cost thousands, probably hundreds of thousands, to fix up, and I'm sure they had other properties in the works too. She's probably got a ton of money wrapped up in this place, and Snaps is her livelihood. She and Owen weren't exactly on great terms when he died."

"What do you mean?"

"Shit," he said under his breath.

"Tyler, what do you mean they weren't on great terms?"

The drone buzzed over the top of the house as he pretended to fixate on the screen.

"Tell me, or I'll ask her about it myself." That last bit was a lie, but he didn't need to know that.

A look of panic washed over his face. "You can't do that."

"Then tell me what you're referring to."

"Fine, but you can't mention any of this to Amy."

I nodded.

He sighed. "Originally, they planned to move to

the house together, but Amy stayed back for a month or so to wrap things up at the apartment. Apparently, one night while they were on the phone, Amy heard a woman's voice in the background."

I felt sick. "You're saying—"

"Owen was cheating on her."

A wave of nausea burbled up from my stomach. "What a slimeball."

"She confronted him, and he admitted the whole thing."

"Why didn't she tell me? Did they try to work it out?" I asked.

Tyler coughed. "They worked it out the first time she caught him cheating a few years back. Maybe she was embarrassed."

I could feel my face go crimson. "He had cheated on her before?"

"Look, everybody's got their own shit to deal with. I don't want you thinking bad things about Owen when he's not here to defend himself."

I pulled away. "I'm thinking bad things about Owen because he was an inconsiderate asshole. Why the hell are you defending him?"

"Because what good would it do to hate him now? He's dead, Robin. He snapped his own fucking neck, and he's dead. Talking about this won't bring him back, and it definitely won't help Amy." His eyes glossed over.

"You're right," I replied. "I—"

"I saw the video," he shot back, his eyes welling with tears. "Before they took it down. I saw him hang himself."

I felt as if the ground had dropped out from under me. "Jesus, Tyler, I—"

"I thought it was a joke at first. When he started recording, he was sitting on the floor in front of the camera, smiling like it was any other video." He twisted around and shoved his hands into his pockets.

I grabbed his arm with my free hand, careful not to bump any of the controls on the remote. "Why didn't you tell me before? I'm so sorry."

"We can be together again." Tyler shuddered.

"What are you talking about?"

"That's what he said. Then he just sat there, smiling and staring into the camera. After a minute or so, he aimed the camera up at a noose hanging from a crossbeam in the middle of the room. Before I realized what was happening, he stepped up onto a chair, hung the rope around his neck, then kicked off." He let out another sob. "He was my friend. I know he fucked up, but the guy didn't deserve to go like that."

I rubbed my hand up and down his back. "No, he didn't. No one deserves to go like that."

"I saw that room yesterday, and it was like watching the video all over again." He sniffled. "I'm sorry. I don't know what's wrong with me."

"Don't apologize. What you saw was awful—the situation is awful. But all we can do is try to help Amy through this."

Tyler pulled away from me.

"What's wrong?" I asked.

He wiped his eyes and stared up into the sky. "Where's the drone?"

I spun around and looked to the sky where the drone had lingered over the top of the house. It was nowhere in sight.

"Shit, shit, shit." Tyler snatched the controller from my hand.

"Can you still see the video feed?"

He tapped frantically at the screen. "It's frozen. Let me try the home button. It'll bring itself back to its starting point." He tapped the screen vigorously.

I held my breath as my ears searched for the sound of spinning propellers. "I can hear it."

He pointed toward the top of the house. "Oh, thank God." The drone appeared from the other side and slowly drifted over the roof. Once it cleared, it descended toward us and landed next to our feet.

Tyler knelt and flipped the switch at the top of the drone. "If it loses connection with the controller or I hit the home button, it'll return to where it started." He lifted it and examined the camera underneath. "Think the camera's fine. Must have just been a bug with the software. It's supposed to stay put when no one's controlling it."

"Maybe the three-thousand-dollar version is more reliable." I nudged him with my foot.

He rolled his eyes. "Funny." He pulled the memory card from the drone and slid it into a plastic case that he shoved into his pocket. After Tyler put the drone safely back in its protective foam—no easy feat, since the propellers had to be positioned in just the right way—we headed inside to check on Amy.

"Thanks for letting me copilot," I said. "Sorry I almost wrecked it."

"It's not your fault," he replied. "I wasn't paying attention either." He lightly jabbed me on the arm as we approached the front door. "But please don't bring up the whole cheating thing with Amy. Let her tell you herself. And she doesn't need to know I saw the video."

I rested my hand on his. "Of course I won't. You're probably not in the mood, but if you ever want to talk about it again, I'm here for you. I can't imagine how you feel."

He nodded. "Thanks."

We found Amy in the living room, frantically scribbling on a notepad.

"Everything okay?" I asked.

Amy glanced at us over the edge of the notepad then continued writing. "I've got so much to do before tomorrow. My parents get here in the morning, and I haven't even started on their bedroom."

"I could take the couch, and they could have mine," Tyler said.

Amy held her hand up. "No, you're not sleeping on the couch. But I could use your help. Between the three of us, we could clear out the rest of the junk in the bedroom next to Tyler's and clean. The room's not in great shape, but they're only staying the night. Then I've got to go to the grocery, clean the rest of the house, follow up on—"

I reached for the notepad. "Give me the list, and we'll take care of it."

Her eyes widened.

"I'm serious," I added. "I can go grab anything we need from the store. Tyler can start on the bedroom, and that'll give you time to wrap up any business stuff. But you have to promise that you're taking tomorrow off. It's Owen's funeral, for Christ's sake. Things won't be perfect around here, but your parents will understand."

Her expression softened. "You're right."

Tyler peered at the list over my shoulder. "This isn't much stuff. We'll have it done in no time."

CHAPTER EIGHT

The death rattle started at the edge of a dream and lingered as I crossed the barrier to the waking world. I lay in bed for a moment, my body warm, almost too warm, under the heavy quilt I'd pulled from the old wardrobe. The mechanical breath came once more, and my heart constricted with each ghostly wheeze. My eyes traced the intricate patterns on the quilt to the edge of the bed. I could just make out the ugly gold mirror as it bounced against the old plaster wall. I pulled the quilt back, and the chill rushed in as soon as I'd left its protective warmth. I reached for my sweatpants on the floor next to me and slid them up around my waist while careful not to break eye contact with the mirror.

At first, I thought I had imagined the sound, but as I stepped closer, the breaths grew louder and the rattle more distinct. The mirror seemed to move in rhythm with each wheezy gasp for air. I listened carefully, half convinced my mind was playing tricks on me. But the sound was unmistakable. My reflection shook as the mirror vibrated against the wall, and I worked up the nerve to grab its frame. The next exhale came with a hot gust from behind the mirror and tickled my fingertips.

"Dad," I whispered, and my breath fogged the mirror's surface. I felt foolish for saying it out loud. When the next breath came, I pulled the mirror loose from the wall.

The mirror had been used to cover a break in the plaster, a three-inch hole laced with uneven wood slats protruding like broken ribs. I set the mirror aside and stared into the black. The next breath brought with it a smell that made me gag—chalky vanilla, like the shakes I used to make him drink when he refused to eat solid foods.

I scrambled to the door and twisted the knob frantically, but something held it firmly from the other side. I backed toward the bed and screamed—at least I thought I screamed—and the door sprang open.

Tyler stood in the doorway, in nothing but a pair of boxers and a ratty T-shirt. He gripped a broken banister rail like a baseball bat. "Are you all right?" He pushed past me and turned the corner to survey the room.

I pointed at the hole in the far wall and inched closer to the door.

"What? What did you see?"

"Just look." My voice quivered.

He reached for the light switch, and the overhead glow rushed in and chased away the lingering shadows. I squinted at the black hole, and it appeared to absorb the surrounding light.

Tyler stepped toward it and ran his fingers along the broken slats. "Did you see a rat or something?"

"I heard him breathing," I said before I could stop myself.

"What?" He tapped the wall with his knuckle and listened. "I don't hear anything. You must have scared it away."

I'd heard my dad. I'd smelled his breath. I realized how crazy it sounded, and I tried to wipe the panicked tears from my eyes and regain my composure. I must have dreamt it. I'd had nightmares like that before—ones where the dream world slipped into my waking brain and projected itself on the walls. I had no other explanation, and I didn't want Tyler to think I'd lost my mind. "You're right. It must have been a rat or a rattling pipe or something. Just caught me by surprise."

He looked at my trembling hands, and I clasped

them together to try to stop the tremors. He opened his mouth as if to speak, but I cut him off. "Look, I need you to do something for me."

"Yeah?"

"I'm a little freaked out right now." I settled for blunt. I'd spent so much of my life afraid of what people would think or of letting people down, but after Dad's death, those trivial fears no longer seemed to matter. "I want to stay with you tonight—in your room."

Tyler leaned against the wall.

"No funny business and no ulterior motives. I just don't want to be alone right now. That's all."

He grinned. "So I'm just your big teddy bear. I see what—"

"No jokes." I cut him off. "You don't have to joke, and you know that's not true."

I think the honesty might have been too much for him, and his grin faded. "I'm not trying to be mean, but I just need for you to do this for me tonight. You don't have to make a joke about it."

"Okay. Are you sure you're all right?"

"I will be," I replied.

He nodded and gestured toward the door. "Let's go."

The chill slipped out from under Tyler's door and ran along my bare feet. "She wasn't kidding when she said it was cold in here.”

Tyler opened the door, and an icy blast followed. “Nope. It’s colder than a witch’s tit.”

“What the hell are you talking about?”

He shrugged. “Something my grandma used to say.”

Although Tyler’s room was freezing, his bed was bigger and looked more comfortable, and his room even came with a crushed-velvet love seat.

Tyler pointed. “I’ll sleep on the couch, and you can have the bed.”

I sat on the edge of his bed. “That’s sweet of you, but that couch is half your size. And it’s not like we haven’t slept together before.”

Tyler suppressed a smile.

“If it’s okay with you, we can share the bed. I trust you,” I added.

“Fine with me. Just don’t scream in my ear in the middle of the night.”

“No promises.”

We lay next to each other and stared at the plaster ceiling.

“Where the hell is Amy?” Tyler asked after a few minutes of silence. “You were shrieking like a raving lunatic, and Amy’s bedroom is right down the hall. She would have heard you.”

"I don't know. Maybe she took a sleeping pill? I wouldn't blame the girl with all she's been through."

I lay there for a few more minutes, but I seemed to have screamed away any chance of sleeping. "You still awake?"

Tyler rolled to his side. "You scared the living shit out of me. Yeah, I'm still awake."

"Thanks for letting me stay with you."

Tyler bit his upper lip.

"What's the matter?" I asked.

"I know you're probably tired of hearing this, but I'm really sorry to hear about your dad."

I averted eye contact. "Thanks."

"Who knows? Maybe you'll get to see him again someday."

I laughed. A few dozen people had said something similar—"He's smiling down upon you. You'll see him again. Yada, yada, yada." It was getting old. "I never took you as the religious type."

"I'm not, but maybe there is something after death."

I rolled my eyes in the darkness. "This is going to sound dumb, but when I was little, after Mom died, I asked Dad what happened after you died. Where did you go? He said he didn't know and that no one could know because none of us have ever been there. He was an atheist, and he was probably just humoring me, but we made a pact. If either of us died before the other, and there was anything after death, we'd turn all the lights on in the house to let the other know we were okay. It would be our secret signal. It was a stupid, childish thing. But the day he died, after the people from the funeral home left and the apartment was quiet—I swear to God if you ever tell anyone this, I'll kill you." I punched him on the shoulder.

"I won't. Finish your story."

"I sat in the dark and waited for him to turn the lights on. And of course, he never did."

"That means nothing," he replied. "Just means dead people can't flip light switches."

I laughed and wiped the corners of my eyes.

Tyler shuffled next to me. "Since we're being honest tonight, can I tell you something?"

"Sure."

"You know how I mentioned I saw the video? Owen's video, I mean."

"Yeah?"

"I can't get it out of my head. I haven't been able to sleep, and all I can see is that grin on his face. It's like he was happy about it. I just don't get it."

Why does he have to be vulnerable now? I swallowed hard, but the truth came bursting forth. "I lied to you earlier. I freaked out because I heard my dad breathing in the room tonight. When I found the hole in the wall, I smelled the gross vitamin drink we used to feed him. It didn't feel like a dream."

His eyes widened. "That sounds awful. No wonder you screamed."

"Death just puts a funk over everything. This place feels like a tomb, knowing Owen died here. I don't know how Amy can stand to stay in this house. And with the funeral tomorrow... I'm dreading it."

"Me too." He rolled over, with his back toward me. I could tell he didn't want me to see his face. "The sooner it's over, the better. I hate funerals."

"I don't know anyone who particularly likes them." That got a chuckle. I scooted up against him and wrapped my arm around his waist. "Is this okay?"

"Uh, sure," he replied.

I never would have admitted it, but I'd slept alone ever since our working rendezvous in Detroit. Hell, I'd slept on a scratchy couch for most of the nights since. When I'd moved into Dad's apartment, the nurse had warned me about what she called caretaker loneliness. "Make sure you take time for yourself now and then," she said. "Go see a movie or go to dinner with your friends. Get out of the house." I told her I didn't have anyone to stay with him. I was an only child, my aunt had passed away years ago in a car crash, and the rest of the family was too distant, either literally or figuratively, to help. She offered to submit the paperwork for a home health aide to stop by for a few hours a week, but that left me with only enough time to run to the grocery store or step out to grab lunch. Maybe Dad had forgotten who I was and didn't care, but the thought of leaving him alone with unfamiliar faces had made me cringe. *What if he dies while I'm gone?* The man had done so much for me. He'd raised me by himself and made sure I grew up into a semi-well-adjusted human. I had no tiny creatures to take care of, just a dad who did little more than sit in bed and watch crime show marathons. I'd thought I could handle it.

But God, I'd longed for the warmth of another human body and someone to confide in. I felt Tyler's abs poking out through his shirt. Either he'd been working out since my last visit to Detroit, or he was flexing—I couldn't be sure. And had we been in that situation a year ago, I might have slid my hand underneath his shirt and slowly traced the line between his abs to his belly button. Instead, I rested my hand on his waist and held close to him as if he were a life preserver and the only thing keeping me from sinking into a bottomless ocean.

CHAPTER NINE

I lay strapped to the operating table, unable to move as the surgeon positioned the bright-white light over my face. I tried to shift my head, but a large metal clamp held it in place. I pulled against the leather restraints as soft music drifted through the room.

"We'll need a sample of the tumor," a voice boomed from overhead. A hand hovered above me, gripping a rusty hand drill. "This should be fine. Did you hose it off?"

"Nah, but we've only used it once today."

"Stop." My mouth moved as if stuck together by globs of peanut butter, and the word came out in an unintelligible slur. The drill disappeared from sight. As the sound of crunching bone echoed through my head, the light became white hot and too much to bear.

I fell through the metal surgical table into a soft

mattress and sheets that were cool to the touch. As soon as my brain stopped blocking signals to the rest of my body, my eyelids shot open. I lay safely in Tyler's bedroom. The overhead light was blinding at first. No wonder I'd dreamed of a surgical table. Every light in the room had been turned on. Tyler must have been a heavy sleeper and snored softly next to me.

I reached over and flipped off the bedside lamp then slid my legs from underneath the covers, careful not to disturb him. As I flipped the light switch on the wall, I heard tinny music drifting underneath the door. I crept into the hallway and toward the landing. The glass chandelier over the staircase seemed to pulse with the music.

Strauss. My heart thumped in my chest. *Metamor-phosen—one of Dad's favorites.* The stairs creaked underfoot, and my palms became clammy as I reached the foyer. The lights, the music, and—a faint whiff hit my nose—the smell of panfried pork chops. I stepped slowly toward the kitchen, sucking in the scent.

He stood over Amy's six-burner stove, a dish towel slung over his shoulder, stirring a pot with one hand and cradling a glass of red wine in the other. He tapped his foot to the music coming from the record player on the back bar. It had been so long since I'd seen him healthy, even in my dreams. "Dad?" The question came out in a whisper.

"Hey, my little chickadee," he said over his shoulder. "Dinner's almost ready. Pour yourself a glass of wine and have a seat." With his spatula, he pointed at the corner of the island that had been set with two place settings.

The music crescendoed as I stepped to the stove and leaned in to see his face. His beard was bright red once more, replacing the sporadic patches of peach fuzz that had clung to his face when I last saw him. The halo of hair surrounding his bald spot had even filled in. His skin was taut and shiny, unlike the loose, inelastic flesh that clung to his bones during his last days.

He glanced at me out of the corners of his eyes—his brown eyes with bright whites, no longer tea stained and lined with spindly red arteries from the cancer treatments. "What's wrong, sweetie? Aren't you hungry?"

"Dad?" I ran my hand over his azure-blue sweater, and the stitches tickled the tips of my fingers.

"The one and only."

"You're dead."

He chuckled. "Hope you won't let that ruin our dinner." He grabbed a plate from the counter next to the stove and slid a pork chop out of the pan, followed by a large scoop of mashed potatoes and a spoonful of peas. "I made the potatoes with cream cheese, the way you like." He held the plate out, and I took it. "Take it to the table, and I'll be right behind you."

I sat on the counter stool, and he twisted around with a plate of his own. His bread belly—the man didn't drink beer—hung slightly over the counter as he plopped onto the stool next to me. He leaned in and lifted my chin with his index finger. "We have little time. I don't want you to spend the entire meal moping." He filled my wineglass. "I want to catch up. Tell me what you've been up to. What brings you to this fancy house?"

I laced my fingers around the stem of my wineglass and took a large gulp then set it on the counter as Dad cut into his pork chop. "I don't know where to start."

"From the beginning," he replied.

I told myself I was dreaming. What else could it be? But we ate together, food that I swore was real. And we talked, not the absurd conversations I'd had in previous dreams but real talk between two actual people. I didn't want it to end. After the meal and a few glasses of wine, Dad looked at his watch. "Afraid it's time for you to go, sweetie. I'll clean up, and you go back to bed."

My eyes hung heavy from the wine and the late night, but his words sent a surge of adrenaline through me. "I don't want to go. I want to stay with you."

He smiled and rested his hand on mine. "You need

to rest. But I'll tell you what. How about we do this again?"

"Tomorrow?" I asked.

He nodded. "Sure thing, chickadee. Now, you head on up to bed."

My chest tightened as my lips uttered ancient words that had become so unfamiliar on my tongue. "I love you, Dad."

"I love you, too, sweetie. Now, go to bed." He grabbed the dishrag from his shoulder and snapped it at me as he rose from the counter. "Before I make you help me clean up."

I stood and wrapped my arms around his waist. "I miss you."

"I miss you, too, darling."

I floated through the hallway toward the staircase, unaware of my physical surroundings. My mind played a tug-of-war, sad that the moment was ending but happy that I'd gotten to see him again. I skipped Tyler's room and headed straight to mine. I wasn't afraid anymore.

CHAPTER TEN

I awoke to the orange rays of the dawn sun casting a radiant glow over the bedroom. The taste of wine lingered on my tongue, and although my stomach usually grumbled in the morning, it gave no audible signs of hunger. For a moment, I wanted nothing more than another dream. I rolled over in bed and stared at the plaster ceiling, trying to relive the postmortem meal. I must have sleepwalked back to my room.

I reached for my phone on the nightstand to check the time—8:13. Amy's family would arrive at any moment, and the funeral was scheduled for one. The thought of another funeral made me want to run from the house screaming, but I needed to be there for Amy. I set the phone down and pulled the covers tighter around me. Just as I reached the edge of sleep once more, the groaning of the doorbell carried through the hallway.

I slid my legs over the side of the bed and reluctantly pushed off onto the floor. The hardwood creaked in the hallway, and Tyler emerged from the second-floor bathroom.

"Hey there," he said with a sly smile. "Where'd you go this morning?"

I held my fingers to my lips. "Would you keep your voice down? All I need is for Amy to think something's up between us."

His smile faded. "Oh, okay."

"And do me a favor and don't tell anyone about it, would you?"

Tyler grimaced, and his eyes shifted to the floor.

"No, I don't mean this—us." *Whatever that meant.* "I mean the hole in the wall."

The corners of his lips lifted. "Can do. I'll be down in a minute."

The bell rang again, and with Amy nowhere in sight, I approached her bedroom door. As I lifted my hand to knock, I heard faint whispering from the other side.

"I swear I'll tell. They deserve to know. It's not fair." Amy's voice was hoarse and panicked.

I tapped on the door, and the whispering stopped.

"Who is it?" she called out.

"Amy, your family's here, I think. Is everything all right in there?"

"Fine. Everything's fine." She sniffled. "Would you let them in? I'll be down in a few minutes."

I looked at my white T-shirt and sweatpants. *At least put a bra on.* I ran to my room to change then headed downstairs to the front door.

Amy's mother stood on the porch, cradling a Crock-Pot in one arm and plastic grocery bags in the other. Her thick fur coat made her look as if she were smuggling an extra casserole or two underneath.

"It's about ti—" She stopped short when she saw me standing in the doorway. "Oh, I—"

"Sorry, Amy's still getting ready. I'm Amy's friend. You must be her mom. I recognize you from her Snaps feed."

"Her what, dear?"

"Just an online thing. Here, let me help you with those bags."

"Her father's waiting in the car." She turned toward the gray SUV in the driveway and beckoned. "Herb, would you get your bony ass out of the car and carry in the other grocery bags?"

Herb pushed the car door open and grumbled. "It's too goddamned cold to be waiting out in the freeze. And you look like a walrus in that puffy thing." His eyes darted toward mine, and he nodded in a brief salutation.

Her mom let out a hearty laugh. "Don't pay any attention to him. He gets cranky from long car rides."

"Me too." *Tyler's going to like them.*

Herb hobbled up toward the front steps. "It's my damn knees. You spend twenty years jumping on and off tanks and see if you enjoy being wedged in a car for two hours."

She rolled her eyes and mimicked the words as he spoke, as if he'd said the same line a thousand times.

I took the Crock-Pot from Amy's mom and backed against the door to let her through. She didn't wait for me to show her to the kitchen but found her own way there, stomping down the hardwood in her scuffed kitten heels.

"This place needs a ton of work," she said as her voice trailed off down the hallway and into the kitchen. "Oh, how stunning."

I held the door open for Herb, who gave me another obligatory smile, barely visible under his thick gray mustache.

I looked into the Crock-Pot as I joined them in the kitchen. *Chili. What a weird choice for a funeral.* I set it down on the counter, next to the grocery bags.

"You must be Robin. I've heard so much about

you." Amy's mom leaned in and squeezed me with her gargantuan arms.

And you must be trying to kill me. "That's right," I replied as my lungs struggled to take in fresh air.

Herb peered over her shoulder. "Let her go, dear. Can't you see the girl's turning purple?"

"Sorry, sorry." She loosened her grip. "I'm Patricia, and this is—"

"Herb," I said, reaching out to shake his hand.

"I'm just so thankful the two of you came to stay with her." Her chin trembled. "We would have gotten here sooner, but I couldn't find someone to cover my shifts."

"Oh?"

"I'm an in-home nurse. Can't just go leaving people to care for themselves." She sniffled.

What are the odds? "I understand. My dad had a home nurse. If it wasn't for her, I'd have had to put him in a facility."

"You poor thing. How is he doing?" she asked.

I looked down at my shoes. "He passed away a few months ago."

Her cheeks flushed red. "But you're so young. I'm so sorry to hear that."

One of my college friends had come out to his parents after freshman year. He told me that ever since, he felt as if he was always coming out—when making new friends or even at the dentist's office when the hygienist asked whether he was married or had a girl-friend. I felt the same way about Dad's death. I was always breaking the news to someone.

"It's okay," I said as if she'd lost my father and it was my job to console her. "I'm doing okay."

Patricia pulled a tissue from her coat pocket and blew her nose. "That's good, dear. I'm glad to hear it, but I'm so sorry for your loss."

Amy emerged from her bedroom and descended the staircase, wearing a simple black funeral dress. Her makeup was polished as if she'd just completed a makeup tutorial, but no amount of eyeliner could hide the fact that she'd been crying. "Hi, Mom." Her voice broke.

"Oh, sweetie, I'm so sorry." Patricia rushed over to Amy and embraced her in a bear hug.

Her father shuffled awkwardly, obviously waiting for Patricia to step aside so he could move in.

I escaped the kitchen and went upstairs to get ready. As I reached my bedroom door, Tyler stuck his head out from the crack of his. His black tie hung loose on his neck and swayed like the pendulum of a ticking clock. He wore his slim-cut suit like a model on the cover of a fashion magazine, not someone who sneaked inside abandoned buildings for a living.

"I'd give them a minute if I were you," I said. "Things are pretty emotional down there."

"Thanks for the warning."

"You look cute for someone headed to a funeral," I said.

His cheeks went crimson.

I went to my room and stared at the black skirt and blazer hanging underneath a plastic dry-cleaner bag. I'd worn the same outfit to Dad's funeral, and it was the closest thing to formal clothing I owned. "I'm burning you after today. No more funerals," I said under my breath, as if the announcement affected the eventualities of the universe. I slipped into the depressing garb and looked at myself in the clouded oval mirror.

"Amy and her parents just headed out. Think you'll be ready in five?" Tyler asked from the other side of the door. "I'll warm up the van."

"Ready as I'll ever be." I gave myself one last look in the mirror, touched up my makeup, then trudged to the hallway.

CHAPTER ELEVEN

Clouds hung low in the sky and pressed down upon me like the lid of a closing coffin. The icy wind cut across my cheeks and carried with it a fine layer of snow that covered my peacoat.

"You're trembling." Tyler offered his arm as we approached the funeral home, and I wrapped my hand around his bicep. "Are you sure you want to go in?"

I swallowed hard. "I'm fine," I lied. Amy had ridden with her parents while Tyler had graciously chauffeured me in his white pedophile van—his words, not mine. As we entered the building, I felt as if I were walking straight through the portal to Hell and Tyler was my only anchor to reality.

"All right, but just say the word if you need some fresh air."

I stood at the back of the room and stared at the

display ahead. A plain cherry box rested atop a slender podium. Baskets of funeral flowers lined the back wall, and a bright arrangement of white roses and chrysanthemums sat next to a framed image of Owen. His parents had chosen an older photo, before the dyed-black hair and raven tattoo that spread across his chest and poked through the collar of his shirt. Had it not been his funeral, I wouldn't have recognized the clean-cut kid in the photo.

"Want to go up and say hi to Amy?" Tyler asked.

"I need a minute. You go ahead."

Tyler gave a sympathetic nod and ambled across the ruby-red carpet toward the front of the room.

I found the only chair not occupied by a family octogenarian and took a seat. I couldn't face Amy, not right away at least. Several people gathered around a TV and watched a slideshow of Owen's childhood pictures. The obligatory bathtub picture became the first day at preschool, then elementary school, and high school. Had Owen graduated from college, there would have been a graduation pic too. I'd found a similar progression of photos in a frame on my dad's desk, one simply stacked on top of the other until the frame's metal bulged at the edges.

"Always wondered why he wanted to punch all those holes in his face." The woman sitting in the chair next to me leaned in, bracing herself on her cane. "But

I guess everyone has their vices." She reached into her purse and pulled out a small flask just far enough for me to see. "You look like you've been hit by a truck. Want a nip?"

I shook my head. "No, thanks. Are you Owen's grandma?"

The woman chuckled. "His great-aunt, actually." She pushed her horn-rimmed glasses farther up her nose. "My sister's a Mormon, so that cuts down on the fun she's allowed to have."

"I'm Robin. It's nice to meet you."

"Doris," she replied.

"I'm sorry for your loss. I don't know how you can stand it."

Her expression softened. "Sweetie, I've been bawling all morning. I'll be pulling tissues out of my shirtsleeves for days." She pointed at the screen. "It's hard to look at pictures of that little guy up there. But I've seen a lot of death, and at my age, I'm much closer to dying than I am to being born. Eventually, you learn to take each day as it comes. Cry when you need to cry, but remember to laugh too. What's the point of living if you can't laugh?" Her upper lip quivered, and she leaned back in her chair. "No one can ever take the good times from you."

Tears welled in the corners of my eyes, and Doris pulled a clean tissue from her sleeve before I had the chance to ask. We sat together for a few minutes, making small talk and looking at the pictures flashing across the screen. I looked toward the front of the room. "I better go up and see Amy, but it was nice to meet you."

"You, too, dear." She pulled another tissue from her sleeve. "You better take one for the road."

My black flats rocked forward but seemed fused to the carpet. I would have to slip through the maze of family and friends to make it to the front, and the thought overwhelmed me.

A hand gripped my shoulder with a reassuring squeeze. "Have I told you how much I fucking hate funerals?" Tyler straightened his tie. "Amy seems to be doing all right. Are you ready to head up there?"

I'd told myself the day wasn't about me and I would have to suck it up for Amy. I was armed with an extra tissue from Doris and forced one of my feet forward. "Let's do it."

Tyler led the charge, taking the brunt of the familial blows as we approached. When we reached the front of the room, Amy's mom blew into a shriveled handkerchief as Herb made awkward conversation with another man I didn't recognize.

Amy's eyes met mine as she hugged an elderly relative. They screamed, *Get me out of here.*

I remembered how it felt, being too exhausted to

cry but having to stand and make small talk with agonized acquaintances while reliving the shock of his death. She still hadn't brought up the fact that Owen had cheated on her twice, and I wondered what was going through her mind, having to grieve for a partner but being furious with them at the same time.

We greeted Owen's parents then shifted over to Amy.

"Oh, thank God." She pulled me close. "I don't know how I'm going to do another hour of this."

She switched to Tyler, who leaned in and whispered something in her ear.

"I knew I could count on you," she replied. "Meet you at the van in five?"

"Sorry to interrupt." Owen's mom leaned in. "Amy, not sure if you've ever met Owen's great-aunt Doris. She's leaving soon, so come meet her before she goes."

"We'll meet you outside," Tyler said.

"What are we going outside for?" I asked.

"A little enlightenment." He patted the breast pocket of his suit.

We slipped through the glass double doors, past the gaggle congregating around the folding table of two-liter drinks, Styrofoam cups, and store-bought cookies. I sucked in the chilly winter air, clearing my nose of a potpourri of different colognes and perfumes from the hotbox of people stewing inside.

"Halfway through," he said as we walked toward the van on the far side of the parking lot.

I'd wondered why he'd parked so far away from the other cars. "God, I remember how it felt. All you want to do is go home and sleep, but you're surrounded by people." I climbed into the van's passenger seat.

Tyler reached inside his jacket pocket and pulled out a thin joint. "You smoke?"

"Today, yes. Yes, I do." I grinned.

He lifted the joint to his lips and flicked the flint wheel on his lighter. Smoke slipped through the crack in the window as he handed me the joint. My head buzzed by the time we'd made it halfway through, but Amy still hadn't emerged from the funeral home.

"I thought she was going to meet us out here," he said.

I took another little puff. "I'm sure she's been pulled aside by some family member. She'd have to pass by all of them to get to the front door, so there's no way she'd waltz right out."

A woman wearing a black funeral dress and large sunglasses crossed the parking lot. She stopped at the edge of the asphalt just before the tip of her heel hit the concrete sidewalk to the front doors. She fidgeted with the slim beige rectangle in her hand then spotted us in the van and headed in our direction.

Tyler flicked the joint across my path and out the

passenger window then waved the pot smoke away. "What the hell does she want?"

She gave a meek wave as she approached. "Are you guys here for Owen's funeral?"

Tyler pointed. "Yeah, it's through the doors on the left."

Her hand trembled as she rested the tip of the beige envelope on the edge of the window. "Would you mind giving this to Amy for me?"

"She's on her way out here if you want to give it to her yourself."

The woman pulled back, and her eyes darted to the front door of the building. "No, I can't stay." She thrust the envelope into the cab. "Please, just give this to her." She gave another panicked glance toward the opening door of the funeral home then rushed back to her car.

Amy emerged cradling her purse under one arm and waving a relative away with the other. A look of relief crossed her face as she approached the driver's-side window. "Not picking up women in the parking lot, are you, Tyler?"

He held out the envelope. "She left this for you."

Amy glanced at the car pulling out of the lot and took the card from him. "Who was she?"

"No idea," he replied. "But she didn't want to wait to give this to you."

Amy scrunched her eyebrows, flipped the card over, and ran her black nail along the seam.

With Deepest Sympathy was scrawled across the front of the card, bordered by blue butterflies and purple lilies. When Amy opened it, a couple of folded steno pages fell loose. She unfolded them and read, her eyes scanning the lines as a wrinkle deepened in her forehead and her smile faded.

"What is it?" I asked.

She folded the card and tossed it into Tyler's lap. "I can't deal with this right now," she huffed. "I'm going back inside."

"Wait," I called after her, but she ignored me, and her heels clomped against the asphalt as she marched toward the funeral home.

Tyler opened the card and straightened the stack of papers inside.

"What does it say?" I leaned over to get a better look.

"Holy shit!"

"What?"

"That must have been the girl who was banging Owen."

"Could you be any cruder? Why would she want to talk to Amy?"

"I don't know, but she's got balls of steel showing up at his fucking funeral." He flipped through to the last page, and his eyes widened. He held the paper out for me to see.

She had underlined the last lines on the page. "You're in danger. Stay away from the house. It's not safe," I read aloud. "What the hell does she mean by that?"

CHAPTER TWELVE

"Has she lost her goddamned mind?" Amy's hand trembled as she took a swig from her wineglass. "How could she have the nerve to...?" She clenched her jaw tight.

I crossed the other side of the island toward her. "Amy, she was freaked out. I don't think she wanted to cause any trouble."

"Of course she wants to cause trouble. What the hell else could she possibly want from me? She's already fucked my husband. Does she want my life too?" She slunk onto one of the island stools and cradled her head in her hands. "I didn't want you to find out about this, Robin. It's so embarrassing."

I shot Tyler an uneasy glance. *Too late.* "You have no reason to be embarrassed. This has nothing to do with you and everything to do with Owen. You didn't make him cheat on you."

Amy gripped the corners of the countertop so hard her knuckles went white. "I know what I'll do. I'll file a restraining order. No. I've already had police snooping around here, prodding and asking questions. You know, they actually thought I talked him into doing it at first? Can you believe it? I had to prove to the police I didn't talk my husband into killing himself. Now, I feel like my entire life is on display for everyone to see."

"Why would anyone think you were involved in Owen's death?" I asked.

Amy scowled. "I'm surprised you haven't seen it yet. Just search for my name. Do you know how many accounts I've had suspended since all of this started? People are posting terrible stuff about me. My husband's dead, and somehow, I'm the bad guy. It's complete bullshit." Her eyes darted to the kitchen window. "Shit, my parents are coming back in." She pulled a tissue from her pocket and frantically dabbed at her running mascara. She pointed at Tyler with her wineglass, sloshing the last few drops of wine onto the counter. "Not a word of this in front of my parents. I'm lucky they didn't see her today. Thank God they don't use the internet."

The back door flung open, and Amy's mom barreled into the kitchen. "Your father and I are going to tackle that backyard before we leave. We'll fill that ungodly hole before the ground freezes and clear all the brush. Then in the spring, we'll come up and help you plant some fresh flowers." She ran her hand through Amy's hair, and Amy let out a loud sob.

I grabbed Tyler by the arm and pulled him into the hallway. "What a disaster. Did you know that people were blaming her for Owen's death?"

Tyler shook his head. "No, I fucking swear. I mean, I've seen a few things on the internet, but I didn't know that she was taking any of it seriously. There's stuff floating around about me too. I just don't pay attention to it anymore."

"She can't keep living like this. Once her parents leave and we go home, she'll be here by herself. She's got a crazy mistress wandering around telling her she's in danger, and the internet thinks she's killed her husband. She's trying to keep her feed going like nothing's happened. She's going to break, Tyler. Maybe not now, but when we leave and she's all alone..." I held back a fresh set of tears.

Tyler folded his arms. "Then we won't leave until we're sure she'll be okay."

"Don't you have shoots planned? You can't just put everything on hold." I thought of my whitewashed apartment and stalled projects back home. "I'll stay with her. You can go back to Detroit, and I'll stay here until she figures out what to do with the house, if she'll have me. It's not like I have anything going on back home. It might be good for me."

"We'll feel it out. See how the next few days go," he said.

* * *

PATRICIA INSISTED on cooking one last meal before they left. I helped Tyler put the leaf in the dining room table, and we set out the dishes Amy had made from clay and fired herself.

"I don't know why you insist on making all this creepy stuff." Patricia examined the spiderweb patterns on a black-glazed serving bowl. "It gives me the creeps." She scooped mashed potatoes from a metal mixing bowl until the other bowl's pattern had been sufficiently covered in starch.

"It pays the bills, Mom. It paid for this house." Amy seemed to take out her rage toward Owen's mistress on the carrot she was peeling.

Her mom, oblivious to the tense energy radiating from Amy's body, shouted into the living room, where Herb sat reading the paper. "I told your father you should take a break from all this dark nonsense."

As Amy swiped vigorously with the peeler, she took a thin strip out of her thumb. "God dammit." She tossed the utensil into the sink and ran her hand under the faucet, leaving drops of blood on the cutting board and kitchen floor. "Would you back off, Mom? My husband died. Could you give me a break from the constant criticism?"

Herb poked his head around the kitchen doorway.

Patricia shrank back and, for the first time since her arrival, seemed to have nothing to say.

I grabbed a paper towel and cautiously approached. "Tyler, get a bandage. I think I saw some in the vanity upstairs."

Amy wrapped her thumb with the paper towel. "I've made such a mess."

"Don't worry about it." I rubbed her shoulder. "Just take care of that cut, and I'll take care of the carrots. I hate carrots, anyway."

Tyler returned with a package of bandages and handed them to me then turned to Herb. "Herb, my man, how 'bout we make a round of drinks?"

Herb's eyes flashed to his wife.

"A lemon drop," she replied as she held back tears.

Tyler cleared his throat. "Well, we've got bourbon and bourbon, so how about a bourbon instead?"

"Fine, fine." She put a timid foot forward as Herb and Tyler left the room in search of booze. "Sweetie, I'm sorry. I didn't mean anything by it. You know your father and I don't understand this stuff, but if it's important to you, that's all that matters." She reached for the bandages, and I stepped aside.

"I know." Amy stood at the sink but refused to face her mother.

Her mom fiddled with the packaging and gently pulled Amy's hand under the light. "It's just a scratch. These peelers will get ya. I shaved my knuckles a few times with them, and it looked like a murder scene. I don't mean to nag, it's just I don't know what else to say. I want to help you, but I don't know what to do." She sniffled.

Amy rested her uninjured hand on her mom's. "I know. I'm glad you guys are here. You're helping just by being here. But back off the career, okay? The *creepy stuff* is important to me." She smiled.

Her mom nodded. "Sometimes, your mom's brain can't keep up with her mouth." She helped Amy with the bandage as I cleaned up the carrot massacre behind them.

Tyler and Herb had set the table with highball glasses, each filled with a healthy amount of bourbon.

* * *

AFTER AMY'S PARENTS LEFT, we crashed in the living room. Amy lay on her back on the black leather couch, staring at the ceiling. I remembered how I felt going home after Dad's funeral. I'd dreaded that moment for days, but once it was over, it felt as if I'd left him behind. I looked at the rest of my life like a ski slope. I'd reached the peak, and the only place left to go was into the snowy abyss—leading to where, I didn't know. Amy might be lying on the couch, but her mind was clearly miles away.

I looked at my watch. *Ten o'clock.* I was exhausted in an I'll-never-sleep-again sort of way. Grief sucked the energy right out of a person but somehow made it impossible to rest. I pushed myself out of the wingback chair. "Tyler, help me in the kitchen."

He looked up from his phone. "What are we doing?"

"We're making popcorn and watching shitty horror movies. Amy, I believe I see your VHS tape collection on the bookshelf over there. Pick one."

"You think she's really in the mood to watch a horror movie?" he asked.

Amy smiled. "I'd love to watch one." She went to the shelf and ran her hand along the aging cardboard boxes. She pulled loose a red-and-white-striped case. "We should start with *Candy Cane Massacre*. It's one of the worst movies I've ever seen."

"Perfect!" I turned toward the kitchen. "Help me find Amy's popcorn."

Tyler joined in as I rummaged through Amy's cabinets. He pulled a box from the cabinet atop the fridge. "I thought you'd given up on horror."

"I have, but a movie might make Amy feel better. I can suck it up for one night."

"You're a fucking class act, you know that?" He pulled the cellophane wrap loose and tossed the popcorn bag in the microwave.

I grabbed a large bowl and set it on the island. "I just remember what it feels like to have the rug pulled out from under you. Only I was too stubborn to ask for help."

Tyler turned toward me. "I don't think you—"

"It wasn't a question. You tried to check in on me a dozen times, and I blew you off."

"Yeah, but Robin, your dad died. You were allowed to do whatever the hell you wanted. I understood. Amy understood."

I ran my palm along the cool granite countertop. "At least Amy is willing to accept our help, and I'm going to be there for her, just like you tried to be there for me. I never said it, but I appreciated you checking in on me, even if I didn't reply. It let me know I wasn't alone."

The microwave dinged.

I wrapped my arms around his side and squeezed then made my way to the microwave.

Amy stood in front of the bookshelf, staring impatiently at the black tape rewinder. "Owen was always terrible about rewinding the tapes. I told him a thousand times that if you're going to watch my tapes, you better freaking rewind them."

Gingerbread creatures marched across the screen, brandishing sharpened candy canes. Santa's sled had been outfitted with dual-mounted machine guns, and his reindeer were zombielike and thirsted for blood. The entire ordeal was hilariously bad, and we'd polished off two bags of popcorn by the time the final credits rolled.

The follow-up film was of the haunted-house variety, an eighties film with puppet poltergeists and a laughable budget.

"Looks like we lost Tyler," Amy said from the couch.

Tyler had made it halfway through the second movie before passing out in the chair next to me. His chest rose and fell as he snored softly.

"Thanks for doing this with me," she added.

"Of course." I yawned.

"I'm sorry you had to find out about Owen cheating on me that way. I was so embarrassed. I just didn't know how to tell you, and you were dealing with your dad."

"Don't apologize. I haven't exactly been available, and I can't imagine how you felt when you found out. I wouldn't have wanted to tell anyone either." I picked at my cuticles. "So, how do you feel? We never talked when you and Owen were going through it, and it must be so difficult being sad over him and being pissed off at the same time."

Amy shook her head. "I gave him so many chances. I just didn't want to throw away everything we'd worked so hard to overcome."

"You mean with him cheating on you?"

She rubbed the back of her neck. "That and other things."

"What other things?" Amy had put up a wall between us for most of my stay. I could feel it, like she was holding something back. But the woman sitting on the couch wasn't the Amy of the last few days. She'd wiped her makeup off, revealing the deep bags and blemishes underneath. I was talking to Amy, not the front she'd so carefully curated.

She glanced over at Tyler, who was still fast asleep in the chair, then looked at me. "I had a miscarriage." Her words came as a whisper, as though if she spoke too loudly, the house itself would hear her secret.

"Jesus, Amy, I—"

"Thank God we hadn't told anyone yet. The pregnancy was a surprise, but he was so excited about it. Losing the baby destroyed him. Destroyed me too. We kept quiet about it, but shortly after is when all the other problems started. I tried to talk to him, but he started pulling away from me. After I caught him the first time, we went to a counselor and attempted to work through it. When he moved into this house, he stopped all effort to deal with it. I knew something wasn't right, but I never thought he'd cheat on me again."

Tears flowed freely down her cheeks, and I reached for a tissue on the end table and handed it to her.

"I tried to hate him." She sniffled. "God, I wanted to hate him so bad, but he was hurting too. Maybe if I'd done something different, we could have—"

"Amy, that's bullshit." My outburst caught both of us by surprise. "He made a choice to be a cheating asshole. It has nothing to do with you. You didn't go running around with another guy."

"You're right. I just wish I'd had the chance to work it out with him before, you know…"

"Have you decided what you're doing to do with the house when you finish it?"

Amy smiled. "I haven't gotten that far."

I lay my head on the chair's headrest. "Well, whatever you decide, you can count on our help."

"That means the world," she replied.

We talked for a while then tried to finish the movie. I sank deeper into the chair until I nodded off completely.

CHAPTER THIRTEEN

I awoke to a blinding light overhead and familiar music wafting into the living room. *Dad must be cooking again.* I followed the musical trail to the kitchen, where he sat waiting at the island.

"I thought I was going to have to come and get you. Your food's getting cold." He smiled. Two plates of pasta sat in front of him, and he reached over with a bottle of wine and filled the pair of empty glasses on the counter. He was less talkative this time and hardly touched his food. Instead, he watched me eat and studied my features as if he were preparing to paint a portrait.

"You seem off tonight," I said. "Everything okay?"

He pushed his plate aside and swirled his glass of wine as he leaned closer. "Something's on my mind."

"What is it, Dad?"

"I've just been thinking. You're only here for a few more days, and then you're headed home. I won't be able to see you anymore." He traced a vein in the marble.

I pushed my plate aside too. "That's not true. You can come and visit me anytime." I realized how absurd it was to argue with a figment of my imagination.

Dad shook his head. "Sorry, chickadee. Afraid I have to stay behind."

Each word hit like a dagger. I didn't want to say goodbye again, even in my dreams.

"But I have an idea." He lifted his head, and his eyes glistened. "How would you like to have dinner with me every night?"

"What do you mean?"

He squeezed my hands. "You could see me whenever you want. Any time of day or night."

I looked at our hands. I could feel his rough skin scratching against mine. His hands were always dry. "How?"

"Stay here with me. We can be together again, in this house."

I chuckled. "But this is Amy's house." I expected the dream to slip into absurdity, or to wake up, but he kept staring. He seemed to feel me slipping away and tightened his grip. "This is my house, chickadee. And we can be together forever. I just need for you to do one thing."

"Anything," I replied. I thought I meant it.

He stood from the island and crossed to the kitchen counter. "Are you sure? You're not going to like it, but it has to be done."

Time was running out. I could feel my mind going fuzzy. "Just tell me! I think I'm waking up."

I heard the metal *shink* of a knife being pulled from the butcher block. He clutched the spine of a chef's knife in his hand. He stepped toward the island and slid it toward me. He smiled wide, and his expression seemed foreign and unfamiliar.

"What do you want me to do with this?"

He rolled his arm over and drew his index finger across his wrist. "Then we can be together, and I'll never have to leave you again. But first, I'll show you my secret place, where no one will find you."

I looked down at the knife on the table then up at him. I thought I'd misunderstood. He couldn't have meant—

"It'll be quick. Just a slash, and it'll take a few minutes at most."

I slid out of the chair and backed away from the counter. "How could you ask me to do something like that?"

"You want us to be together, don't you?" He frowned.

"I'm not doing it. What the hell is wrong with you?"

His expression drooped, and his eyes narrowed, as if he were a child who'd just had his favorite toy taken away.

"I've got to go." I didn't know where to. *Back to my room? Where do you escape a dream?*

I pushed past him, but he grabbed my wrist. "Wait, don't go. I'm sorry. I'm just so lonely here. I don't want you to leave me. Won't you just stay with me a little while longer?"

I couldn't refuse him. It was a dream, after all, and my dreams had a tendency of getting away from me. It wasn't his fault. It wasn't his dream.

I rested my hand on his. "Sure, Dad."

"Tell me a story." His eyes lit up.

"A story?"

"Like the ones I used to tell you when you were little. I'm sure you have them all memorized by now."

I thought of the green book sitting in my car. "Sure, Dad. I'll tell you a story."

I awoke in Amy's wingback chair, with Tyler still out cold in the chair next to me. The couch where Amy had lain was empty. I stretched to chase away the ache in my back and crept to the kitchen. Aside from a plastic popcorn wrapper, the kitchen was pristine. I walked to the butcher block and pulled out the chef's knife. *The horror movie got to you*, I told myself as I slid the knife back in.

I tiptoed to the foyer, eager to nab another hour or two of sleep in a non-vertical position, and crossed the rays of morning sun that cut through the room. I stepped carefully onto the outer edges of the steps to reduce my chances of waking Tyler. As I reached the second-floor landing, I heard whispering from Amy's bedroom.

"How could you ask me to do that?" Amy's voice was weak and trembling.

I knocked softly and held my breath as I waited for a response. But Amy remained quiet on the other side.

I reached for the handle and pushed.

Amy sat on the side of her bed with her head cradled in her hands. I hadn't seen her room before, but it was a disaster. Clothing racks lined the walls, and the clothes for her Snaps photo shoots hung in tangled clusters, some dangling loose and threatening to fall free. Laundry was strewn across the floor in sporadic piles, and empty plastic bottles and wrappers were stacked on her nightstand. Her comforter lay on the floor, and she sat on a bare mattress.

"Is everything okay?" I knew instantly that it was a stupid question.

She twisted around. "What are you doing in here?" Her expression shifted from fear to anger. "Didn't you even think to knock?"

"Amy, I—"

"Get out!" she yelled.

I backed toward the doorway, slipped through, then pulled the door closed behind me. I stood on the landing, unsure of what to do, my neck hot with embarrassment.

CHAPTER FOURTEEN

I lay awake, staring at the plaster cracks in the ceiling and too mortified to face Amy. Eventually, I abandoned sleep altogether. Thoughts swirled in my head—guilt for bursting in on Amy earlier and thoughts of Dad sliding the knife across the table, its cool metal blade reflecting his sick smile. The previous day played through my head like a movie of someone else's life, a life that felt foreign to me. How awful it must have been for Amy to be accused of Owen's death while trying to mourn it. The thoughts and emotions swirled until they were replaced by a feeling I was all too familiar with—unbearable emptiness.

I grabbed my laptop from the nightstand and flipped it open. She'd mentioned online trolls and banned accounts, but I'd been offline for so long I'd missed the drama. I typed Amy's name into the search engine. Her pale-white face popped up in the results. The first pic was from Amy's apartment Halloween party, when her account had first blown up. In the thumbnail, she stood next to a spindly black tree constructed from dead branches and speckled with orange bobbles.

I scrolled down the list of search results, but all led back to her accounts and websites. I added *conspiracy* to the search bar and pressed Enter. My index finger hovered over my laptop's track pad.

Social Media Influencer Accused of Driving Husband to Suicide.

I clicked the link that took me to an ad-riddled webpage with an embedded video. I clicked Play, but *This video has been removed for violating our Terms of Service* appeared instead of the footage I'd been looking for.

I followed the search results, and each seemed to lead to the same banned video. After a few minutes of browsing, I finally found a page with a video that had escaped the culling. I held my breath and clicked the thumbnail. I wasn't sure what I was getting myself into but was relieved to find the clip was audio only.

I immediately recognized Owen's voice.

"I'm sorry for all the pain I've caused, Amy."

His voice made me shiver. The audio must have been ripped from his final recording. It had been so long since I'd last heard him, but he didn't sound sad or distraught. He sounded relieved.

"Now, we can be together again."

Agonizing silence followed before the narrator's voice cut in. "We've boosted the volume, and if you listen carefully, you'll hear a voice in the background."

A static hiss came from my laptop speakers, and I reduced the volume so no one would hear me from the hallway.

"Do it." The statement punctuated the white noise. I flipped the lid of the laptop closed and tossed it to the end of the bed. A wave of nausea worked its way up my esophagus. I pulled out my phone and sent Tyler a text, sure he was still asleep in the armchair downstairs.

Come here.

His phone dinged from the first floor, and I waited with bated breath for the symbol that indicated he was typing.

Come where?

To my bedroom.

He replied with a winky face, and the floorboards creaked as he crossed from the living room to the staircase. Tyler tapped on the door. I twisted the knob and pulled the door open a sliver.

"What's up?" he asked with a grin.

I pushed him back so I could peer around the corner toward Amy's room. Her door was shut.

I pulled Tyler inside. "You cannot say a word to Amy about what I'm going to show you."

His smile faded. "Okay."

I gestured for him to sit next to me on the bed and grabbed my laptop. "I heard Amy talking to herself again, while you were asleep in the chair."

"Again?"

"It happened yesterday morning, too, after her parents arrived and I went to check on her. This time, I opened the door. She got really angry with me for barging in. And I felt so terrible about it that I haven't been able to sleep."

Tyler rested his hand on my shoulder. "You're babbling. Just tell me what's going on."

I took a deep breath and opened the lid of the laptop. "I've been researching. Amy said they'd questioned her about Owen's death."

"Yeah, that's pretty normal, I assume."

I shook my head. "But she mentioned that people thought she'd made him kill himself. That's not normal."

Tyler looked down at the bed.

"I found one of the videos. They enhanced the audio from the beginning of Owen's suicide video."

The blood drained from Tyler's face. "And?"

I refreshed the page. "Are you sure you're up for this? It's just the audio but..."

Tyler ran a hand through his hair. "Just play it before I change my mind." His eyes glossed over when Owen's voice came from the speakers.

I listened carefully for the boosted voice. The whisper was feminine, but it was impossible to tell if it belonged to Amy. "Do it," the voice said several times, quietly goading Owen to take the next tragic step. The audio cut out, and the narrator's voice cut in.

"That can't be real," I said again under my breath. It had to have been some kind of internet hoax. "Someone could have easily edited the footage to make it sound like there was another voice in the room." I pulled out my phone and flipped through Amy's Snaps profile. "There's no way she could have done it." I held out my phone to show him the photo in her profile. "She was doing a shoot that day and wasn't even in town."

"And that's probably why the police dropped the investigation."

"Then whose voice was it, Tyler? You heard it just like I did."

"It's just someone playing a cruel joke is all. Just anonymous assholes on the internet."

I scrolled the video notes. "Maybe, but this is extreme." I noticed a link at the bottom of the notes. "They included a link to the original audio."

"Don't waste your time with this stuff. Owen's

gone, and there's no sense dredging all this up. It won't bring him back."

My tired mind had frayed at the edges. He was right. I had been trying to distract myself from the fact that Amy was pissed with me and had allowed my brain to go down a dark internet rabbit hole. Just as I reached to close the laptop, a thought wormed its way out of the darkness. "What if it was the mistress? You can barely hear the voice on that recording. It could just as easily have been her. And couldn't you import the file into one of your fancy production programs and tell whether someone had messed with it?"

"Maybe. If audio was pulled from the original video, it should be pretty obvious if someone tampered with it. But I'm sure the police have already looked into her too."

"Then it'll turn out to be a fake, and we'll never discuss this again. But wouldn't you rather have the peace of mind?"

Tyler shrugged. "If it'll help you sleep, I'll look. Send me the link. And if it turns out to be nothing, and you force me to listen to that tape again, you're going to owe me big-time."

CHAPTER FIFTEEN

Tyler stood in the doorway to my bedroom with his backpack slung over his shoulder. He pressed his lips into a thin line. "Go for a ride with me." It wasn't a question.

"Everything okay?" I peered over the edge of my laptop screen.

Tyler stepped back into the hall and double-checked his periphery as a stand mixer whirred on the first floor. "I just want to grab a coffee." He forced a smile.

"I think we've still got some good stuff left. I—"

"Just come with me, won't you?" His fingers fidgeted against his jeans.

"Yeah, sure," I replied, "although I'm not sure coffee is the best thing for you right now. You seem a little on edge."

He cocked his head to the side and gave a look that said, *Just shut up and do this for me.*

I put my laptop on the nightstand and slipped on a pair of flats.

"I'll drive," he said as we took the stairs to the first floor.

The mixer shut off as he opened the front door. "Come look at this!" Amy called into the hallway.

I opened my mouth to speak, but Tyler grabbed my arm and pulled me through the front door.

"What the hell's wrong with you?" I asked as I steadied myself on the porch.

He pressed his index finger to his lips and waved me toward the van.

A fresh dusting of snow had left patches of bright white on the front lawn, and my flats slid on the gravel drive as I approached the passenger side of the van. "The weather's supposed to get worse, isn't it? Are you sure you want to leave now?"

He ignored me and climbed in then gripped the van's steering wheel so tight his knuckles went white. The van's back wheels slid on the thin layer of fluff as he eased out of the front drive and onto the street.

Serious wasn't a look Tyler often wore, and it unsettled me. The last time I saw Tyler serious was on a short expedition to an abandoned carnival park during my visit to Detroit. I'd followed him and his small crew through the area, and a squatter had pulled a knife on us. "What's wrong? You're freaking me out."

"I'll show you once we get to the coffee shop. I found something."

"Amy's going to be pissed that we just left without saying anything to her."

"Amy will be fine." He'd chewed on his bottom lip so much a thin line of blood ran across it. "Trust me."

"And you couldn't have shown me at the house? Mysterious."

His head snapped toward me. "I'm not fucking around, Robin."

I opened my mouth to speak but settled on silence. My efforts to break the tension had only made things worse.

He drove across town until we reached a small coffee shop nestled next to an old Methodist church. He grabbed his backpack from the back of the van, and we headed inside. The place was buzzing with the chatter of college students and amateur novelists.

Tyler bolted for an empty table in the corner of the room, and I followed close behind.

"Don't you want a coffee?" I asked.

He gestured toward the empty seat across from him. "Coffee can wait."

I slipped into the chair as he unzipped his back-pack and pulled out his laptop. "I looked at the audio file. I found the voice in the original file they posted too. I'm not an expert, but I couldn't find any signs it had been added in after the fact. You can barely hear it, but it's there, and it looks like it's been there all along."

My stomach went queasy. "So whose voice is it? Amy was out of town. It could have been the mistress, but—"

"It's Amy. I don't know how, but she's the one egging him on. Maybe she was on a video chat or something but—"

"That's crazy. The police would have figured that out, don't you think?"

Tyler shrugged. He opened the laptop then scrubbed across the track pad. "I was looking through the drone footage from the other day, and I saw something." He flipped the laptop around and clicked. "When we lost the drone, it drifted to the back side of the house and captured something on video."

As the drone lowered over the roof, it scanned the expansive slate tiles then the brambles in the backyard. At first, the drone looked as if it were about to plummet to the ground, but at the last second, it snapped around, probably as Tyler tapped the home button on his phone. As it rose to the sky, the drone caught the back side of the house. The paint on the back door was chipped and peeling, and the brick needed repair.

"Did you see it?" he asked.

"See what?"

Tyler sighed and flipped the laptop around. He scrubbed once more then twisted the screen around for me to see. "Standing behind the kitchen door."

Just before the drone lifted above the house once more, it caught an image in the backdoor window. I leaned in and squinted.

"It's Owen," he said.

I pulled back from the laptop. "What are you talking about?"

"Just look at it," he replied.

The figure appeared to be male, with short black hair.

"It's probably just a weird reflection." I blinked hard and looked at the image once more. It definitely appeared to be human, but I'd seen enough shadowy ghost photos to know that shadows and dust particles could make convincing specters.

"It isn't a reflection. Owen isn't dead. She's fucking lying to us. They're lying to us." He scrubbed once more until the frame sharpened.

It was unmistakably Owen.

"What can I get you?" the server took a pencil to her order pad, clearly missing the tension hanging in the air.

"We're good for now," Tyler said.

"You've got to order something if you're going to

take up a table." She scowled and tapped her order pad.

"Just two coffees," he shot back.

She rolled her eyes and stormed off.

"That doesn't make any sense. We saw his urn at the funeral. He's dead. How could he have faked it?" I asked.

"I don't know, but who's standing in the window? This is all some big hoax. How do we know the police were ever involved? We didn't see his ashes in that urn."

My mind reached for a memory from the morning of Owen's funeral. "When I heard her whispering, the day of Owen's service. She said something about needing to tell us—that it wasn't fair she couldn't tell us."

Tyler's eyes widened. "She's fucking scamming us. I don't know what kind of sick game they're playing. I don't know how she faked the funeral. Maybe it's some big gag for Snaps or something, but Owen's hiding in the house."

"Why would they fake his death?" I asked. "How awful—to tell his family that he died. How could they even think of putting someone through that?"

Tyler leaned in. "Do you realize how much press that video got? Owen flipped haunted houses for a living. If their marriage was crumbling, a stunt like this would keep their business afloat, and I bet people would be eager to buy the place."

"She seems oddly fixated on her Snaps feed, but she's not psychotic." I crossed my arms.

"Then how do you explain Owen standing in the window? That's him. He's not dead."

I put my elbows on the table and massaged my temples. "What do we do?"

"We pack up our shit and get out. I'm not gonna be a part of their game."

"We can't just leave. We should at least ask for an explanation."

"And what could they possibly say that would make you want to stay? 'I'm sorry, we just felt so bad about your dad's death, we thought it'd make you feel better if we faked Owen's. Misery loves company.'"

His words sucked the air out of my lungs, and I blinked hard to squelch a fresh tear. "Now you're being an asshole." I scooted back in my chair and stood, momentarily forgetting that he had been my ride there and I had no way home without him.

"I'm sorry. I didn't mean it like that." He reached for my arm, but I pulled away.

"Robin, wait."

"I'll be in the van." I snatched his keys from the table and headed toward the door. I sat in the van and waited for Tyler, mulling over the situation. I shouldn't have called him an asshole. I wasn't sure what was true anymore. When he emerged from the coffee shop a few minutes later double fisting two to-go cups, I reached over and pushed the driver's-side door open for him.

He gave me a side-eye and handed me a coffee. "I'm sorry. This is all just a lot to take in. If you want to confront her, I'm up for that. I just don't think she's got any valid way to defend it. And if this whole thing blows up in her face, we don't want her dragging us down with her. This is my career we're talking about."

I laughed. "You've still got one of those?"

"Don't joke. You do too. Once you get the shop up again, things will go back to normal."

"Not sure I want things to go back to normal," I replied.

As Tyler drove to the outskirts of town, I found my mind consumed by thoughts of Owen living secretly in the house. *His parents think he's dead. How could he do something like that?* By the time we reached the drive-way, I was fuming. Tyler's anger seemed to have rubbed off on me.

We went inside and found Amy leaning over a molded chocolate skull, carving the outlines of a set of teeth with a sculpting tool as her head bobbed to music blaring through a Bluetooth speaker. She looked up from her chocolate creation. "Aw, why didn't you tell me you were going to get coffee? I could have gotten something."

Tyler pulled his laptop from his bag and set it on the island with a thud.

"What's gotten into you guys? You leave without saying anything, and you both look like someone just peed in your cereal."

Tyler flipped the laptop around and pointed at the center of the screen. "Who the fuck is that, Amy?"

Subtle.

Amy leaned in, and her eyes widened as they darted between Tyler and the screen.

"It looks like—"

"Don't play dumb. We know he's still alive. Now, tell us why the hell you'd do something like this. Where is he?"

Amy's eyes scrambled to mine, but I shifted my gaze to the tile floor. "Wait, what are you implying?"

"That Owen's not dead. That you faked his death and he's hiding in this goddamned house."

Amy's eyes glossed over. "Why would I do something like that?"

"I don't know," Tyler replied. "Followers? Press."

Amy shrank back as her expression shifted from one of fear to anger. "How dare you."

"Just tell us why you're doing this."

Amy lurched forward and stuck her index finger in

Tyler's face. "You didn't find his body, Tyler. You didn't cut him loose from the ceiling joist. I had to tell his parents. Do you know what that's like? To tell a parent their kid's dead?" Her voice trembled. "Finding his body was the worst moment of my life, and telling his family was a close second." Her head snapped toward me. "Do you believe this bullshit too?"

"Whoever's in the video looks exactly like Owen," I mumbled.

"And you think I'd be so desperate—so sick—as to fake my husband's death?"

A wave of nausea burbled up from my stomach. Either she was a fantastic actress, or she wasn't acting.

"What about the whispering?" Tyler asked. "Both of us have heard you whispering at night. Who are you talking to? And who was telling him to 'do it' repeatedly in the video?"

Amy's eyes widened. "You've been snooping on me. Now you're buying into conspiracy theories about me?"

"Tell us what's going on, Amy. Who was in the video? Why are you whispering at night?" Tyler's face was so red it looked as if he'd developed an instant sunburn. He backed toward the hallway. "Don't lecture us. You fucking lied about Owen's death. He's in the video, and you're covering it up. Do you think we're expendable? That our feelings don't matter?

What about Owen's parents? You think this stunt is worth their pain?" He said some other words after that as he trailed down the hall, but they came out in unintelligible angry slurs.

I stood with Amy in the kitchen, my feet frozen to the tile. The silence pulsed against my chest and made it difficult to breathe.

Amy looked up from the floor, her face red and puffy. Her voice came out in a squeak. "You wouldn't believe me if I told you. You'd think I was crazy."

"Try me," I replied.

She backed against the counter. "I've been talking to Owen."

She might as well have punched me in the stomach. "So Tyler is right? What the hell's wrong with you? He's hiding? He's alive?"

Amy shook her head. "Not alive. But since he died, he's been coming to me at night. He's still in this house. It's like I can feel him here. I see him in my dreams. They feel so real. And if you caught it on video, it means I'm not imagining him. You've seen him too. I don't know why, but his spirit hasn't left." She bit her lower lip. "I know this all sounds so crazy, but I don't know how else to explain it. You can check his death certificate if you don't believe me."

"I don't know. This is all too much." I wanted to believe her. *But ghosts?* I might have made my living from creepy-crawly things that went bump in the night, but it was all fantasy. I didn't actually believe any of it.

Amy locked eyes with me, and she smiled as if she'd recovered a long-lost revelation. "He says your dad is here and that you've been talking to him. Owen made me promise not to tell that I was talking to him. He said no one would believe me, but how else can I convince you?"

The hair on the back of my neck stood on end. "How could you possibly know that?"

She grabbed my hand. "Robin, they are here with us. This house somehow brought them back."

My hands trembled, and Amy squeezed tighter. "I know this sounds insane, but I can tell you believe me. You've talked to him, haven't you?"

"Yeah, but it was just a dream. I've had dreams of him for months now. But it's not real."

"It is real, Robin. They are here. I know this is unbelievable, but I don't want you guys to go. Can't you talk to Tyler? I need you here." Amy slunk back to the counter stool and wiped her eyes. "Please try to talk to him."

When I knocked on his bedroom doorframe, Tyler was cramming clothes into a duffel bag. He looked up at me, his face still flush with anger. "Why aren't you packing?"

I crossed the room and gently pulled the duffel bag handle from his hand. "Sit down."

"I'm not staying here a minute longer than I have to. Owen's probably listening to us right now."

I shook my head. "Owen's dead. Just sit for a minute."

Tyler looked pissed, but he obliged. "How can he be dead? We caught them red-handed."

I swallowed hard. The words about to leave my lips were insane. "I think Owen's haunting this house." I repressed the urge to laugh at myself.

Tyler scrunched his eyebrows. "What the fuck are you talking about?"

"She says that he's been coming to her at night. I'm not sure how we caught him on camera. Tyler, I've been having dreams about Dad too. But they're so realistic, like he's here. I haven't told Amy anything about them, but she knew."

The color drained from Tyler's face, and he avoided eye contact.

"Please, don't think less of me for believing her—"

"I've had dreams too."

His statement caught me by surprise. "What dreams?"

"Ones that felt so real I wondered if they had been."

"What did you dream?"

He seemed to think for a moment then shook his head. "I can't..." He grabbed his backpack and rifled through its contents. "But Owen's fling—her card mentioned that Amy was in danger. At first, it seemed like a threat or like the girl had lost her mind, but do you think it could have something to do with the dreams and Owen's death?"

I thought back to the knife on the kitchen island. Dad had wanted me to do it, to take the knife to my wrists. I'd thought it was a dream gone wrong, like Owen's suicide had somehow injected my happy dream with despair. But the questions remained. *Why did Owen kill himself? Why did Dad want me to do the same?* "I think we should talk to the mistress." The words came out before I'd fully thought them through. "If there's any truth to this, maybe she'll be able to help. She left her number in the card, didn't she?"

He nodded. "Amy won't like it, though." He cracked his knuckles and stared at his lap as if having some grand internal battle.

"Amy isn't going to find out. We go see the mistress, and if it turns out to be nothing, we won't tell her."

Tyler looked up at me. "If it turns out to be nothing, then it means that she's duping us."

"Then we pack up and leave. Let them have the house and their lies. But I don't think she's lying. How can you fake a death in the twenty-first century? She'd have to have paid off the police, the funeral home. I just don't see how it's possible. And we can't forget the Lady in White. This place has a history. Maybe there is something sinister going on here."

Tyler shook his head. "Then let's pay this mistress a visit."

CHAPTER SIXTEEN

Tyler parked his van across the street from the mistress's small one-floor cottage, and we sat and stared, each unwilling to make the first move. The quaint house sat in odd contrast to the grim situation. White trim and a tall wooden trellis accented the home's cheery yellow siding. Blinds obscured the house's interior, aside from a small hole that had been broken out by the Maine coon feline perched in the front window. A curved stone flower bed stuck out of the snow, and a small evergreen had been planted by the front steps. Decaying pumpkins sagged and slumped on the front porch, their jagged jack-o'-lantern teeth curved inward in rot-ridden smiles.

I looked out at the snow drifting up the woman's driveway. "What the hell are we doing here? This is a terrible idea." The question was rhetorical, and Tyler gave a sympathetic chuckle.

"If it goes poorly, Amy never has to know," he said. "We'll get back in the van and drive away."

What if Amy is right? The thought had been eating at me. *What if some part of Owen was left behind and dinners with Dad have been more than dreams?* "You're sure this is the place?" I knew it was the place. I recognized the car in the driveway from the funeral home parking lot but held out a minuscule hope that somehow, we'd wound up in front of the wrong house with the same car. The thought of knocking on the door made me lightheaded.

"This is it," he replied.

If someone had passed us, two strangers staring out of an unmarked white van, they might have thought we'd come to burgle the place. Tyler made the first move and reached for the door handle. Cold air rushed in with a fresh dusting of snowflakes that melted as soon as they made contact with the van's interior.

We passed a planter of long-dead marigolds as we approached the front door. I looked around at the rotting pumpkins and piles of dead leaves blown up against the front porch. The mail slot was crammed full, and it looked as if the mailman had finally given up and started stacking letters inside the screen door.

"Doesn't look like she's been handling Owen's death well either."

She had a name—Becca Wright. And fortunately—or unfortunately, as was still to be determined—Becca was eager to talk. I had been routed to a voicemail box the first time I called the number inside the sympathy card, but she answered on the second attempt.

Tyler lifted his finger to the buzzer, but the door opened before he had a chance to push it. Becca pressed her face through the crack in the door. "Thanks for coming." She opened the door wider for us to come inside.

The house was a disaster. Blankets formed a human-size cocoon on the couch, a pile of dishes sat neglected in the kitchen sink, and a thin layer of cat hair covered the floor.

Becca looked nothing like the woman who had walked nervously across the parking lot. Her large funeral sunglasses had hidden the deep bags under her eyes, and her hair, previously pulled back into a neat ponytail, hung in a tangled mess against her oversized hoodie.

A flash of gray shot through the doorway and into the kitchen, leaving a fresh trail of hair. "That's Ollie," Becca said as she led us to the dining room. "She's a little timid."

Tyler held in a sneeze, and his red eyes confirmed the reason he didn't have any cats back in Detroit.

Images, printed pages, and news clippings covered the dining room table. My eyes scanned the chaotic piles of documents. "What exactly are we looking at?"

Becca sifted through a stack next to me and held out a printed text conversation. "This was the second to last time I ever talked to him."

I skimmed the page.

She leaned against the table. "He's breaking it off with me. He said he and Amy were getting back together. He said they'd made up. But I know him. He wouldn't do that. He loved me. They were going to split up. He promised me." She pulled a tissue from her pocket.

Tyler rolled his eyes. "Did it ever occur to you they were actually getting back together?"

Becca balled her fist. "Don't you think I considered that? I called him. He sounded strange, and I could hear her in the background, whispering to him like she was telling him what to say."

Tyler shook his head. "Amy wasn't in town when Owen died."

Becca slammed her fist into the table. "I know that. She posts everything to that goddamned Snaps profile. What she's doing. Who she's with. What she's eating for breakfast."

Tyler furrowed his brow. "Then how could she possibly be involved?"

Becca's eyes widened, and she leaned in close as if someone might overhear their conversation. "It was the house," she whispered.

"How could it have been the house?" I didn't mean for it to sound as if I thought she was insane, but that was how it must have sounded.

She folded her arms. "I know. It sounds crazy. I can't stop thinking about how crazy it sounds." She leaned over the table and picked up a newspaper clipping. "But the house has a history." She held the story out for us to see. *Ghost Hunter Makes Grim Discovery.*

"The Lady in White," I replied. "Amy told us all about it. They found the body. But Amy said there hadn't been any more activity since they removed the remains."

"She left something behind," Becca spat. "Something that got ahold of Owen."

"But that doesn't go with the story. The Lady in White—"

"Tell me a story," Becca whispered.

I stopped cold. "What did you say?"

"Tell me a story. That's what it whispered to me. Through the walls, in my dreams. Tell me a story." She whispered the phrase again. "It's why I had to leave him. I didn't want to, but it wouldn't stay out of my head. It wanted me to stay. The house wanted me to stay. And when it couldn't have me, it took Owen instead."

"My father wanted a story. He asked for it. I didn't know what he meant." *That is, when he wasn't trying to convince me to kill myself.* I could only assume it had done the same for Becca.

Becca rushed toward me. "It's after you too. You can't go back to that house. Eventually, it won't let you leave."

I yanked my hand away. "But what does this have to do with the Lady in White?"

Becca stepped toward the table and shoved a stack of papers to the side. As half sheets and crinkled print-outs slid off the edge and onto the floor, she gripped a crudely drawn family tree from the pile.

"She had a son. I tried to talk Owen into coming with me, into getting out of that damned place. But he shut me out. So I started digging, hoping that I could find something that would help. The woman had a son from her first marriage. I found the wedding announcement that mentions him in the newspaper archive. But after her death, there's no trail of him anywhere. No property records, no weddings. He must have been a teenager when she died, but it's like he just vanished. I found no death certificate. I don't think he ever left the house."

"What are you suggesting?" I asked.

"He's still in the house. Something happened to him, just like his mother, and he never left. And I think he's got something to do with Owen's suicide. I think he's playing with us."

Tyler fidgeted with his jacket zipper then looked at me out of the corner of his eye. "I need to tell you something before I lose my nerve."

"What is it?" At that point, I wasn't sure anything would surprise me.

"It's about the dreams I've been having. I didn't tell you who was in them."

"Who?"

"You. The dreams have all been about you. It's like it knows that we... that I still have feelings for you."

Blood rushed to my cheeks. "What did it want you to do? Did it want you to kill yourself?"

Tyler swallowed hard. "No. It wanted me to kill you. It said that if I killed you, we could be together, that we could both stay in that house forever." He glanced out the window. "God, this is so fucked up. I can't believe I'm telling you this." His head snapped around toward me. His eyes were still red from the cats but had gotten worse, tinged by something other than allergies. "I just thought it was some stupid dream gone wrong. You know I would never do that, right? Hell, I wouldn't have even mentioned it, but it wanted a story too. I told it—you—that I would never hurt you, so instead, it asked for a story."

"You said that Amy wasn't planning on moving in and that she was trying to find a way out of her relationship with Owen, right?" I asked.

"Yeah, but what does that have to do with anything?" He sniffled.

"What if the house never wanted Owen? It talked him into something awful, but what if this was all just a ploy to get Amy to move in?"

"I'm not sure I'm following."

"The house wanted Becca to stay. When she pulled away, it gave up on her and focused on Amy instead. Owen's suicide was just a way to get Amy to the house."

Tyler's mouth hung open. "But why?"

I shook off a shiver. "I don't know, but the longer we wait, the deeper it's going to dig its hooks in. We've got to get back to Amy and get her the hell out of that place."

CHAPTER SEVENTEEN

A thick pile of fluff sat atop the dim gas lamp in Amy's front yard. The wind blew harder, sending a vortex of white flakes across the hood of the van. Snow had accumulated on the front steps of the house and clung to the cracks and crevices of its intricate woodwork. I scratched at my cuticles while Tyler stared out the driver's-side window.

He rested his hand on mine. "Are you okay?"

I looked over at him but couldn't find the words. *Of course I'm not okay.*

"What the fuck are we going to do?" he asked.

"We go in, grab Amy, then get out. Seems pretty straightforward to me."

Tyler swallowed hard. "You know I love all this creepy shit, but this is too much. I never thought any of it was real, you know?"

"I feel the same way. But we've both heard the tape and had dreams. We saw Owen in the window."

Tyler swiped through his phone screen. "I can spring for a few nights at a motel while we figure out where Amy's going to stay."

I locked eyes with him. "Thanks for doing this with me."

"Of course. We can't just leave her—"

I grabbed his arm and leaned in. His lips were softer than I'd remembered, shockingly so considering the cold weather and the fact that he'd been biting them for most of the morning. We lingered for a moment, forgetting the outside world and all the uncertainty waiting for us through the front door. For a second, I was back in Detroit, before Dad became ill and the world became complicated.

He pulled back. "What was that for?"

"If you go back to Detroit after this, I don't know when I'll see you again. I don't want to end up wondering what if. I feel like I'm a shell of who I was. I've already given up so much, and at some point, it's got to stop. When we get Amy out of this place—if we get out of this place—let's go on a real date."

I noticed a flash of vulnerability that he quickly hid with a smile. "Yeah, definitely. I would fucking love that."

I gripped the door handle. "Let's go."

Tyler nodded. "And remember, don't go killing yourself and we should be fine." He grinned wide.

I rolled my eyes.

The heavy wind blasted my hair back and forth as the frigid chill from the winter storm sent thick snowflakes down the neck of my jacket.

We found the front door unlocked, as we had left it, and the sound of our shoes stomping on the entryway rug echoed off the foyer walls.

"I was starting to worry." Amy's voice caught me by surprise.

She sat in the sitting room, the one behind the door Tyler had told me to keep closed, in the room where Owen had hanged himself.

Tyler looked as if he might vomit. "Sorry, it took longer than expected."

She stared at the ceiling and swirled amber liquid in her cocktail glass. "Do you need any help?"

"Help?" I asked.

"With the groceries. Are they still in the van?"

I'd forgotten all about the lie, but Amy asked as if she knew where we had gone.

Tyler jumped in. "There was a wreck on the way to the store. Traffic was backed up, so we decided we'd just order in tonight."

"Huh." Amy lowered her head and finished her drink. "Where did you really go?" The fire crackled in the fireplace behind her. She must have been roasting from sitting so close to the flames. "Did you go to see *her?*" Her eyes narrowed.

Tyler gave me an uneasy look.

I took a deep, uneven breath. "Amy, there's something wrong with this house. It's—"

"This house is the only thing keeping me afloat right now," she shot back. "Do you know how many followers I've gotten since I started back? I've gained at least another twenty thousand in the last few days. They love this place. I'm even working on a new brand deal. It'll pay for most of the—"

"This house made Owen kill himself, Amy. It wanted you here, so it set a trap. This place is evil, and we have to leave while we still can." I spoke with certainty, although I was anything but certain.

Amy pulled a bottle from behind the chair and poured another glassful. "You just want to separate us. Owen told me where you two went. He told me you never wanted us together in the first place."

I clenched my fists. "You know that isn't true. And I'm not sure whoever you're talking to is Owen. Or at least, he isn't the Owen you knew. The house is using him against you, just like it used you against him."

Amy scowled. "What do you mean?"

I kneeled next to her. "We listened to the audio from Owen's tape. We heard the voice telling him to *do it.* It's your voice on the tape, Amy. The house was imitating you somehow. Owen's mistress said as much. We have to leave this place. This house is getting to you. It's getting to all of us. It got Owen."

She shook her head. "I won't leave him."

"He tried to talk you into killing yourself, didn't he?"

Tears trickled down Amy's cheeks. "It was just a dream. That's all it was."

"You're contradicting yourself. It wasn't *just* a dream. Tyler and I are having dreams too. If we don't leave now, eventually, we won't be able to. Let's pack our bags and get the hell out of here."

Amy took another swig from her glass then stared at the ceiling once more. She dabbed at her eyes with her shirtsleeve. "Just let me have one more night with him, and we can leave first thing in the morning."

"No fucking way," Tyler said from behind. "We're loading our shit and driving to a cheap motel where the worst we'll have to worry about is bedbugs. I'm over this ghost shit. The house wants us dead. We can't spend another night here."

Amy shook her head. "I'm spending one more night with him. You two can go, and I'll meet you in the morning. I'm not asking for your permission."

Tyler folded his arms and turned toward the staircase. "Fine. Robin and I are out of here. I'm getting my fucking bag," he said over his shoulder.

I chased him up the staircase and through his bedroom. "I'm not leaving her behind." I knew what it felt like to be on an island, and evil forces or not, I wasn't leaving Amy to fend for herself. "We'll leave first thing in the morning. We can take shifts sleeping if we have to, but if we leave her, we're never going to get her out of this place. Don't you see how she's watching the ceiling?"

Tyler scowled. "How can you even consider staying the night?"

"Because I know how she feels. We have to do this for her. If we leave, who knows what she'll do? We can't force her to go with us."

He picked up a pile of clothes and crammed them into his bag. "Then we'll call the fucking cops."

"And say what? She's an adult who wants to stay in her own house. We just have to keep an eye on her and make sure she doesn't do anything stupid."

Tyler shut his eyes and balled his hands into fists. "Okay, I'll stay the night, but we're getting the fuck out of here first thing in the morning."

I wrapped my arms around him and squeezed. "Thank you. We'll stick together and will be fine."

He let the hug linger. "I'll believe you tomorrow when we're on our way to a motel."

When we returned to the sitting room, Amy remained planted in the chair.

"We'll stay the night," I said, "but you have to promise to come with us tomorrow morning."

"Promise," Amy replied with a somber smile.

Tyler crossed his arms. "At least I've got a half a bottle of bourbon left. And it's all mine."

Amy held up her empty glass. "You *had* a half bottle of bourbon. Sorry."

The shutters slapped against the side of the house as the storm intensified. Even though we'd ensured all the intact windows were closed, a draft cut through the place as if the walls were made of paper.

Tyler searched the cabinets and found another bottle of whiskey that Owen must have stashed for a rainy day. "Have to stay warm," he said as he popped the cork.

We had turned on every light in the house, but pockets of darkness remained, and I stayed close to the others in the sitting room and clung to the protective glow of the fire. I tried to get Amy to talk about the future, and after a little whiskey, she seemed to loosen up.

Tyler tipped the bottle to his lips. We'd given up on glasses completely at that point. "Once we're out of here, we'll do another collab—run a special issue of

Urban Rot and feature all the houses you've flipped so far."

Amy nodded. "And we can even feature the trailer I'll have to live in because all our money is wrapped up in this place." She took the bottle from Tyler and swigged.

He looked to me for a life preserver.

"You know you've got us, right?" I asked. "If you need a place to stay, my one-bedroom might be a little cozy, but we can make it work."

Amy looked into the bottle. "I suppose I could still have a crew come in and fix the basics. Maybe I could sell it and recoup a little of the money."

"It's going to be okay," I said. The thought of Amy selling the house to other unsuspecting victims made me sick to my stomach. Innocuous ghosts were one thing, but this was something else.

Her smile was thin. "I'm sure it will be."

CHAPTER EIGHTEEN

A shrill violin screech woke me. I was alone, and the fire had gone out. The lights in the hallway seemed to pulse with the music that blared from the kitchen.

Time for dinner. I pushed myself up from the chair. *Wonder what's on the menu?*

As I stepped into the hallway, a soft moan came from upstairs.

"Dinner's ready, chickadee!" Dad shouted.

I followed the trail of shrieking music to the kitchen. An acrid stench assaulted my nose as my feet hit the hardwood landing. Smoke wafted from the stove, accompanied by the smell of burned meat. I held my breath as I entered the haze.

Dad faced the stove, his figure a silhouette against

the smoke cloud that spewed from the pan in front of him.

"Dad?"

His head cocked to the side violently as if he'd suffered a sudden spasm. "Have a seat, chickadee. We need to talk."

"What's wrong?" I asked as I approached, squinting from the smoke before putting my hand on his shoulder.

He jerked away and slammed the metal spatula on the edge of the stove. "I said have a goddamned seat!"

I backed away. "I'm going back to bed now."

"Not before you have dinner." He spun around. His mouth hung slack to one side as if he couldn't keep it completely closed. "Don't you love me?"

I slid to the other side of the counter, trying to put space between us. "Of course I love you."

He pulled the skillet off the stove and limped to the pile of dirty dishes on the island. "Then why do you treat me this way?" He tipped the edge of the skillet, and a clump of burned black sludge fell onto the first plate. "You don't realize how hard I've worked to make dinner for you, chickadee." Another glob hit the second plate and splashed over the edge onto the island. "Have a seat."

"I'm leaving." I backed toward the hallway.

His eyes narrowed. "You'd like that, wouldn't you?

Just run away and flush everything I've done for you down the toilet." He lifted the skillet over his head and brought it crashing down on the island, sending shards of broken china skittering across the marble and onto the floor.

"I'm sorry. I didn't mean to."

"You never mean to," he shot back. "You certainly didn't mean to let me sit there and rot in that hospital bed." He yanked out a clump of red hair from the side of his head, leaving a patchy bald spot. As he stepped toward me, his face sagged under the overhead light. "If you'd had your way, you'd have left me to die. You practically did." His feet twisted inward as he dropped the cast-iron skillet on the floor. He limped toward me, slouching, his fingers twisting at unnatural, arthritic angles.

"I did my best," I replied, too terrified to move.

"Not saying much. You've been a failure at everything else, so why not this too?"

"That's not fair."

"And you think this is?" He flung his arms to the side, his skin flapping with nothing inside but a few brittle bones. "You think I wanted this?" Tiny objects plunked against the hardwood, and as I looked closer at the dingy yellow pieces falling to the floor, I realized some of his teeth had come loose.

"What do you want?" I asked.

He smiled at me, mostly gums with crooked yellow teeth sticking out like tombstones from mounds of pink earth. "Leave Amy be. If you don't want to stay here with me, fine. Get the fuck out of my house and leave us alone." His lips curled.

This wasn't my father. *This* was the house. The thing was wearing my dad like a cheap Halloween costume. "And if I don't?"

His expression soured, and he lunged toward me, his bones clicking and clacking as I ran for the foyer. I gripped the front door handle, but it was locked tight. As the thud of uneven steps pounded the floor behind me, I raced up the stairs and noticed a light coming from underneath the door to Tyler's bedroom. "Help!" I screamed as I twisted his doorknob.

Tyler lay on his back.

I traced the slender leg straddling him to the thin womanly frame rocking back and forth on top. Long brown hair hung in her face, moving rhythmically against her shoulders. Tyler's glance shifted rapidly between me and the figure on top of him, and his mouth contorted in horror.

She slowly twisted her head, and I faced... me.

"Why so surprised?" She—I—asked. "This is what you wanted, isn't it?" Her head jerked to the side, and her lips slid into a smile. She pushed her tongue out toward me and with it, a ball of writhing maggots.

Tyler screamed as the clump fell on his chest and squirmed apart.

"Leave us alone, chickadee," someone said from behind. "You've had your chance. Now, get out of our house."

I twisted around, and my eyes met the clouded orbs protruding from Dad's withered face.

My chest tightened, and with all the courage I could muster, I grabbed him by his moth-eaten sweater and pressed my face close to his.

"You're not my father. And we're not leaving without Amy."

"Very well, then." The stench of his foul breath slithered its way up my nostrils—it was the smell of spoiled vanilla protein shake. With no teeth left to support them, his lips had sunken inward. He grabbed my shoulders with his thin, spindly fingers and slammed me to the ground.

The floor seemed to drop from under me, and for a moment, I hung in a sea of darkness until my body hit the floor. The impact woke me. I must have rolled off the chair and onto the hardwood.

Tyler lay at an awkward angle on the love seat and bolted upright. "What the fuck, what the fuck, what the fuck?" He scrambled to his feet and frantically wiped the invisible remnants of his dream from his body.

His eyes said it all. "Did you have the same—? What the fuck was that, Robin?"

I held my hands out. "It's just a dream. That thing can't hurt us."

He swiped his hand through his hair. "Where is Amy?"

"You're not my father."

"What did you say?" Tyler asked.

"That wasn't me." I scanned the room for the source of the sound.

"You're not my father." The voice came again, as if broadcasting from the walls themselves.

Tyler pointed at the fireplace.

"You're not my father." The voice echoed off the tiled hearth, rising in pitch and on loop as if the chimney had been filled with overeager parrots.

The vines on the fireplace twisted and writhed as wooden tendrils pulled free from the mantel. One of them shot toward Tyler and wrapped itself around his arm. "Get it off!" He tried to pull himself free as the plants worked their way toward him.

I gripped the wooden vine and tried to twist it free from Tyler's arm. A sharp pain radiated through my hand, and I pulled away. My palm had been sliced down the center, and needlelike splinters protruded from my flesh.

The vines twisted and wrapped themselves around

Tyler's legs, and a loud snap was followed by his help-less yelp.

He locked eyes with me. "Run!" he said through gritted teeth. But I couldn't leave him.

"Pull!" I shouted as I knelt and yanked on the ends of the vines.

He yanked hard and pulled free, leaving a shoe as a sacrifice to the hungry wooden tendrils. He ripped his hand free from the pulsating vines and pulled them loose from his neck, leaving bits of flesh behind. Tyler gasped for air as the vine loosened. As soon as they'd relinquished their grip, he stepped forward and fell to the floor, letting out a pained gasp as his leg twisted at an odd angle.

I crouched next to him and, without hesitation, stuck my head under his arm and tried to lift him. "Can you walk?"

He gritted his teeth and leaned against me, using his free hand to push off against the end table. "I think so." We stumbled to the door and into the entryway.

I'd never felt so relieved to feel the freezing sting of winter's embrace. We fought against the wind as we scrambled down the porch steps and waded through a foot and a half of heavy powder.

Tyler pulled his van keys from his pocket and unlocked the doors. As soon as the doors closed, he slammed his palms against the steering wheel and let loose a train of obscenities.

I let him rage. I might have screamed, too, had I been able to catch my breath.

I rolled my hand over to check the wound on my palm. The splinters that had laced my hand were gone, and the bits of flesh I'd left in the house had been restored. I flexed my fingers to make sure my eyes weren't playing tricks on me. "My cut's gone." I held my palm out for Tyler to see.

His scowl faded, and he ran his finger along the spot where the gash had been. "This doesn't hurt?"

I shook my head. "What about your leg? It sounded like the vine had nearly snapped it off, but you made it all the way to the van."

Tyler lifted his pant leg up and examined his shin. "Doesn't hurt at all. I don't get it. I swear it was broken."

The lights in the house went dark, as if someone had puffed them out in a single blow. The mansion looked like an abandoned vessel afloat amid a sea of white.

"The house is playing tricks on us. We have to go back in there," I said.

Tyler rubbed his temples. "What if it's too late? What if she's..."

I replayed the events of the last few days. "The

dreams, Owen, our injuries—none of it is real. It's like we were stuck somewhere between a dream and real life."

"It sure as fuck felt real," he shot back as he ran his hand along his throat.

"Think about it. The only way the house could cause any harm is when it talked Owen into..." No matter how many times I said the words, they still made me sick to my stomach. "Amy's made it this far. I don't think she would do anything drastic. If the house wanted to kill her, it would have killed her already. If she'd already done something to herself, then why would the house want us to leave so badly? It has her to itself, but it knows that we can still save her. If she was gone, then why would it care about us?" I reached for the door handle. "We can save her, and there's nothing the house can do to stop us."

Tyler reached into the back and pulled out two large utility flashlights. "I'm sure it's going to try."

CHAPTER NINETEEN

The wind whipped through the house's dark corridor as Tyler and I entered the foyer. I expected a spectral fight or at least more imaginary tendrils slithering from the dark recesses of the room. But the house stood quiet, cold, and dead. Perhaps it had already gotten what it wanted. The storm pulsed against the structure, causing the walls to creak and groan around us.

I peeked through the front window and into the driveway. "If we don't leave soon, we'll be snowed in."

"Amy!" Tyler's voice echoed through the foyer, but the house sat unflinching.

I rested my hand on the banister. "I don't like this. She's freaked out and emotional. We shouldn't have agreed to stay. What a stupid idea." Tears welled in the corners of my eyes. I knew that Amy wasn't the type to hurt herself. At least, I thought I knew that. But the darkness took people indiscriminately. Owen was outgoing and resilient, and somehow, it had claimed him.

Tyler shuffled toward me then stopped as if he wanted to comfort me but was too afraid.

I hugged him hard and buried my head in his chest while holding back a sob. "It's okay. This house is fucking with us, Tyler. Let's just find Amy and get out of here."

We walked the halls together. Like any good horror enthusiasts, we knew that separation meant death. We checked the second floor. The mattress in Amy's bedroom had been overturned onto the floor, and clothing was strewn about the room as if she'd fired it from a T-shirt cannon.

Tyler crossed the room and looked out the balcony window. "She's not out there either."

We crept through the hallway, going from bedroom to bedroom, but found nothing more than dusty furniture and rooms in desperate need of renovation.

"Amy!" I shouted once more when we returned to the first floor. I told Tyler, "Let's check the kitchen."

A sickening crack came from the sitting room, like the snap of a leather whip. Owen's body hung in the doorway. His head slouched at an odd angle, and the rope creaked as he swayed back and forth.

The color drained from Tyler's face as he backed toward the front door. "I can't," he muttered. "Not again."

"It's not real," I whispered. I grabbed Tyler's arm and pulled him toward the kitchen. "Just don't look at him."

"You could have saved me." Owen's voice was low and garbled as the rope cut off the flow of air to his windpipe. His body lurched in my peripheral vision, but I dared not look in his direction.

Tyler stopped cold. "I can't..."

"It's trying to get in your head. It's not real, Tyler." I tugged.

"You knew we weren't happy. I needed a friend, but you were too busy—too selfish—to help."

"Shut up, shut up, shut up!" I shouted as I dragged Tyler closer to the kitchen.

Tyler pulled away and stepped backward toward the sitting room and Owen's body. "I'm sorry."

Before he could reach the door to the sitting room, I slipped in front of him and slid it shut. "It's going to say whatever it needs to get us to leave." I placed my palms against his cheeks. "We just have to stay focused."

Tyler nodded. His eyes were wide and puffy. I'd seen countless terrified expressions in horror movies, but nothing had prepared me for the real-life terror splashed on Tyler's face.

"So now you want to forget us." A voice carried from the other end of the hallway. "Just move on with your lives like we never even existed." My father stood at the end of the hall. He looked like himself again, not the saggy sack of bones covered in loose skin.

I swallowed hard and stepped toward him. "It's all fake. Obviously, it doesn't want us to go into the kitchen."

My father's expression softened. "You've been watching too many of those awful movies. It's me, chickadee. It's always been me. I just want us to be together again. I don't know why you have to fight me."

I cautiously approached with Tyler close behind. "You just want to be together again?" I asked.

He nodded. "It's all I've ever wanted."

I lowered my shoulder and charged. My body made contact with empty space. I spun around and faced Tyler. My father had vanished. I waved Tyler on.

The kitchen looked as it had before, but the fridge had been shimmied away from the wall.

"How the fuck did she manage that?" Tyler asked.

I leaned over the counter and stuck my head in the dark space behind the fridge. "There's something back here. It looks like a door. Give me a hand, would you?"

The fridge squealed against the tile floor as Tyler and I worked together to pull it farther from the wall.

"What is it?" I asked as we stared at the odd-shaped cutout in the wall. It reminded me of a small elevator shaft, and two lengths of rope ran vertically through the center.

"It's a dumbwaiter. I've seen these in old houses before. They used them to send food to different floors. She must have had just enough room to slip in." He stuck his head into the shaft and looked up. "Looks like the cart is on the second floor. It must run up into your bedroom."

"I don't remember seeing a door like that upstairs."

"Neither do I," he replied.

"Should we take another look?" I turned toward the hallway, but he grabbed me by the hand.

"Call her," he said. "Maybe she left her phone on."

I pulled the phone from my pocket. "I doubt she's in a talking mood." I scrolled through the faces on my phone screen and tapped Amy's. The phone rang. "At least she hasn't turned it off." I waited and waited for an answer, but eventually, the call went to voicemail. "No luck."

Tyler smiled. "Call her again."

"Why?"

He held his fingers to his lips.

I sighed and tapped Amy's face once more.

Tyler returned to the dumbwaiter and stuck his head into the shaft. He pointed up at the second floor.

We'd heard Amy's ringtone a hundred times that week—"People Are Strange." I held my breath and listened. The faint sound of a piano and electric guitar echoed down the shaft. "I hear it."

We took the stairs one final time, and I followed closely behind Tyler. I called Amy again, and the song came from the doorway at the end of the hall—my bedroom. As we walked toward it, the song grew louder although still muffled as if it were coming from the house itself, pumping through the air vents like spectral elevator music.

I stopped at the door to my room and listened to the music coming from the other side. Tyler gripped the door handle, but I reached for his hand. "I'll go first." He pulled back, and I twisted the glass knob.

I scanned the room for Amy, searched underneath the neatly made IKEA bed frame, and checked the closet crevices. Amy was still nowhere to be found.

Tyler examined the mirror against the far wall. "It's coming from behind here."

A chill ran up my spine. "Of course it is." The smell of Dad's fetid breath came rushing back, and my stomach soured. "Pull the mirror off."

Tyler shot me a worried look over his shoulder.

"Go ahead," I said from behind.

He lifted the mirror free and set it next to the circular hole. I fully expected a blast of fiery breath and the smell of protein shake, but the hole simply stared back like a dying eye. I pressed the call button one last time, and music came from the darkness.

Tyler knelt, his hands shaking slightly, and shined his flashlight into the abyss. "There's something back here."

CHAPTER TWENTY

I stood in front of the festering hole with my sweaty palm wrapped tightly around the wooden handle of a claw hammer I'd found in Owen's toolbox.

"Are you sure about this?" Tyler rested his hand on my shoulder and squeezed.

"Yeah, unless you want to take a ride in the dumbwaiter. But you won't fit, and I'm sure as hell not crawling inside that thing."

The first blow of the hammer sent a tremor through the plaster wall, forming a spiderweb of cracks at the point of impact. I struck again, this time taking off one of the jagged wooden slats that protruded from the break. The plaster gradually fell away, revealing straight wooden laths that reminded me of the underside of a mattress frame. The hammer bounced off the slats, and after several whacks, I managed to crack only a few. "This is going to take forever."

"Think I saw a sledge in one of the bedrooms. Might be time to bring out the big guns." Tyler disappeared from the room and returned a few minutes later with a sledgehammer. I stood back as he swung from behind, bringing its head crashing into the wall and opening the small hole into a gash several feet long.

I held out my hand to stop him from swinging again. Against my better judgment, I stuck my hand through the split and cleared the loose bits of wood, cobwebs, and dust. My fingertips met solid wood on the other side. I grabbed my flashlight and aimed the beam inside. Dingy avocado-colored wallpaper lined the hidden wall, and I noticed the inset of a door, just a foot or so to the left of the hole. "I think there's another room back here."

I stepped back, and we edged out a crude rectangular outline that lined up with the door on the other side. The door itself had been covered with the same ugly green wallpaper. The daisies adorning the wallpaper looked as if they'd shriveled and died over time, their bright-white flowers crusted over by years of dirt, grime, and who knew what kind of animal and insect debris.

I traced the door's edge until I found the doorknob, or at least where the doorknob should have been.

Someone had removed it. As I leaned in, I pressed my ear against the door.

"Do you hear anything?" Tyler asked.

"Whispering. Amy's in there. She definitely went up the dumbwaiter. Can we take a knob from another door?"

"Can do," he said as he disappeared around the corner.

I tapped my knuckle against the door. "Amy!"

The whispering stopped for a moment then continued once more.

"Amy, we're on the other side. We're going to get you out of there."

The whispering continued.

Tyler returned from the hall. "Found a screwdriver."

"Something's wrong with her. I'm sure she can hear me, but she won't respond."

"Just give me a sec, and we'll get her out of there." Tyler pulled the knob free from the hallway door and handed it to me. "Let's just hope the thing isn't locked."

I set my flashlight on the floor next to me and took a deep breath as I pressed the rod of the doorknob into the empty slot and twisted. A plume of dust choked me as I pulled the door open. The air on the other side was stale, as if no one had been inside for lifetimes.

The beam from Tyler's flashlight scanned the

wall, flashing past cases of old books until it came to rest on a rocking chair at the far side of the room. Amy sat with her back to us, slowly rocking back and forth.

"Amy." I stepped deeper into the room, and the temperature dropped several degrees. A candle flickered on the table next to her, and I noticed the other end of the dumbwaiter framed in the far wall.

"Nibble, nibble, gnaw. Who is nibbling at my little house?" Her clouded breath caught the light.

I recognized the line from *Hansel and Gretel*. "Amy, we've got to get you out of here," I said.

"But he wanted a story."

I felt Tyler's presence behind me and gestured for him to wait outside. I continued the approach. "Amy, we just want to help you. This house... it's playing games with us. It's using Owen against you, and it wants to trap you here. I know it's hard to believe, but it lured you here."

"I'm fine. You can go. I want to be here," she replied blissfully. "It just wants to hear a story."

"What wants to hear a story?"

"The baby."

The door slammed shut behind me, extinguishing the candle with its powerful gust.

I wasn't sure what a heart attack felt like, but the pounding in my chest must have been close. "Tyler, open the door!" I shouted as I pounded my fists against it.

Banging came from the other side. "It's stuck. I can't get it open."

I turned to face the black. "Amy," I said into the darkness.

"Nibble, nibble, gnaw. Who is nibbling at my little house?" I felt the warmth of her breath against my face.

I pushed Amy away, and glass broke as she stumbled and hit the floor.

"You won't take them away from me." Her voice was low and guttural. "I've already lost them once, and I won't lose them again."

"Amy, Owen is gone. Your baby is gone. I know it's awful, but this house can't give them back. Please come with us." I cried hot, panicked tears.

"I can see the way you've looked at me ever since I told you. You pity me. Why do you think Owen cheated on me? Why do you think he tried to get away from me? He couldn't handle it, Robin. But he's here now. We're all here. The house is giving us another chance. And I won't let you ruin it."

I pressed myself against the door and looked at the small sliver of light sneaking through the crack underneath.

"Why do you want to take them away from me?"

she asked through a sob. "Why do you want to take my baby away? He wants his mother."

"Amy, I—"

"I won't let you take him!" she screamed. Her black form lunged toward me, and I dodged to the other side of the room, frantically looking for something with which to defend myself. I felt the dumbwaiter next to me. I couldn't wait for Tyler to break through. I sat at the edge of the dumbwaiter and scooted inside. I pulled my legs up and reached for the rope. The pulley squealed to life as Amy approached, grunting and mumbling to herself.

My arm stung suddenly, and a warm trickle ran down my forearm toward my elbow. Amy reached inside and swiped again, but I kicked hard, and my foot connected with her body. Her weapon clattered to the floor. When I made it midway down the shaft, I tried to catch my breath as the stale air sat heavy in my lungs.

She jerked the rope above me, causing the dumb-waiter to shift unexpectedly upward. I grabbed the rope hard to stop it, and it scratched and burned as I yanked in the other direction, leaving needlelike threads in my hands. The house might not have been able to hurt me, but Amy was a living, breathing danger. For a moment, I thought she'd given up the fight, but she'd only stopped to grab her weapon and started to saw at the rope. Panic set in as I tried desperately to get to the kitchen before Amy cut the dumb-waiter free and I careened to my death. My spirits lifted as the light from the kitchen broke through the dumbwaiter cart. But just as I reached for the edge, the rope snapped.

CHAPTER TWENTY-ONE

The wood cracked and splintered around me as the cart hit the bottom of the shaft, and an explosion of pain was followed by a deafening silence. I exhaled, puffing out stagnant air and dust. I must have fallen straight past the first floor and into the basement. I landed on a cast-iron pulley that pressed itself into my back. I was still in one piece, as far as I could tell, but the immediate relief was replaced by something else. As I sat in the darkness, my ass sore from the impact and my arm surely cut in a way that a simple bandage couldn't fix, I felt the presence of another person.

"I know who you are," I told the darkness.

"Of course you do, chickadee. We've had many a lovely dinner together." Dad's voice came from the black, a voice that had read me stories and lulled me to sleep a thousand times.

"You can stop pretending. You're not my father," I spat. I hated the thing for bastardizing my father's voice and for giving him back only to take him away again.

"That may be, but you have to admit that you wanted to believe it. And had you gone along, you could have seen him every day. We could have stayed together. But Amy listened. She told me stories. She missed her baby, so I gave it back to her, just like I gave your father back to you."

"But he's not real," I replied. "He's just a—"

"Fairy tale? A story? An illusion?" the voice asked. "I've heard you all. I know what you need. So I told you the story you wanted to hear. I created the world you wished for so desperately."

"I know about your mother. I know that something happened to you here. But it's not Amy's or Owen's fault." I slowly scooted to the edge of the shaft and pulled myself up out of the wreckage of the dumbwaiter.

"But *they* took her from me. They dug her bones from the earth and left me alone, sitting in the darkness. So I took your friends. I won't be alone again. If I can't have my mother, then Amy will suffice. And in return, she can have her baby."

"What the fuck are you talking about? Amy's not your mother, no matter how much you want her to be." I scanned frantically for a staircase, but the darkness was all-consuming.

"You don't even care, do you? You want to take her away, too, and leave me all alone in this house, just like *he* did."

An eruption of flame cast a bright-orange glow against the far wall of the basement. I stepped over bits of broken wood and approached the flame-spewing metal monstrosity. The door to the basement opened, casting a spotlight from the ground floor, like the sun breaking through a patch of clouds after a thunderstorm.

I slid into the shadows as a pair of shoes clomped against the old wooden steps.

"My father was a good man. He loved me," the voice said.

A man appeared, dressed in a pair of black trousers held up with suspenders over his white dress shirt. He rolled up his billowing sleeves and grabbed a shovel from the base of the steps as he approached the giant metal box.

"Don't worry, girl. He can't see you," the voice said.

I wasn't willing to risk it.

The man leaned over and jammed the shovel into a black heap on the floor. He shoveled black into the flame and shielded his eyes from a renewed burst of heat.

A coal furnace.

Before I could fully grasp the situation, he let out a low grunt and clutched his chest. He fell into the coal pile, and a puff of black shot into the air as the flames from the fire died completely.

"Unfortunately, his heart gave way when I was just a boy."

Screaming came from the top of the stairs. I slowly approached the staircase and rested my hand on the edge of the railing.

"My mother married again. Another businessman. His heart was stronger but made of the same stuff that we used to heat the house."

The tunnel of light washed the darkness from my skin as the stairs creaked under my feet. I recognized Amy's first-floor hallway, only it seemed as if I'd stepped back in time. The floral wallpaper, once peeling and water damaged, looked like it had just been slapped on the walls. The wood finishes were flawless and shiny, and the blemishes in the old hard-wood had vanished completely. I followed the source of the sound to the sitting room, the same room where Owen had killed himself.

"The boy is a monstrosity! He isn't fit to see the

light of day, and I will not have him tarnishing my reputation. He's costing me clients!"

I poked my head around the corner. A man towered over the woman in front of him. The chain of his pocket watch bounced against his vest as he thrust his finger in her face.

She backed against the wall, scrunching the fabric of her wide-skirted dress against the wood panels. "He hasn't been outside for weeks. He just wants to go to the park. He won't bother anyone." Her voice wavered.

"If you take him, take your luggage too. You know how I feel about that wretched thing."

Her eyes glossed over, and her jaw went slack as she turned away from the man. But before she could reach the hallway, he grabbed her arm and yanked her back to face him.

"Do you understand me?" He brought his face a mere millimeter from hers.

She averted her eyes. "I understand," she said softly.

He released his grip, and she rubbed her wrist as she took the staircase to the second floor.

"Follow her," the voice goaded.

I knew where she was headed. I trailed her down the hallway to my bedroom.

The false wall was missing, and a boy lay on the floor

in the secret room, his head down in a novel. His body wasn't quite right. He favored his right side, and his left leg was shorter than the other. His left hand was clawlike, as if his fingers had melted together. The woman watched him from the doorway as he hummed softly to himself.

"I wish you wouldn't do that," he said, his voice teetering dangerously close to the edge of puberty. "I can't concentrate when you watch."

She wiped a tear from her eye and cleared her throat. "A mother can't watch her little boy now and then?"

"I'm not little," he shot back with a hint of contempt.

She smiled. "You're quite right. I can see you growing before my very eyes."

The boy appeared to think for a moment then slid a bookmark in between the pages of his book and flipped it shut. He glanced over his shoulder, and for the first time, I saw his face. His forehead bulged on the left side, so much so that it had consumed his left eye. His nose was small and crooked, and his teeth sat at odd angles behind his puffy lips. His right eye was a brilliant shade of green. "Can we go to the park?"

His mother took a step back. "Not today, I'm afraid." She sniffled another tear away.

The boy cocked his head. "What's the matter?"

"Nothing, my boy."

"Tell me a story, then," he replied.

She crossed the room and took a seat in the rocking chair. "It's the least I can do. Which story would you like to hear?"

"The one about the witch in the woods."

As the boy pushed himself to his feet, a shrill scream came from behind me. I turned to see his mother lying in the center of my bedroom floor, her head haloed by a puddle of blood. Her husband stood over her, his hand clasped to his mouth. His head snapped to the doorway as if he were looking right at me. "Look what you made me do, you bastard!" He rushed toward me, and I tried to shield myself from him. But instead of attacking, he gripped the door hard and slammed it shut.

"He buried her in the yard." My voice came out in a squeak.

"I watched from the window," the voice replied.

I eased toward the window and stared down at the five-foot-long hole in the backyard.

My mind flashed to Dad's funeral, standing over the grave and watching them lower the casket. The feeling of fear and uneasiness in my gut faded. I felt sorry for the boy. I grieved for him.

A loud bang on the window caused me to jump, and I shielded my face from the shattering glass. I opened my eyes and watched as the wooden window frame twisted and splintered. Bricks cascaded in from the sides, sliding across the window frame and piling on top of each other.

"The last time I felt fresh air was the day my step-father buried my mother."

The final brick slid into place, bringing the room back to darkness.

"I'm so sorry," I whispered.

"He made a new family, and I was their deep, dark secret, too, for years. He left me for weeks at a time, with just enough food to ensure I didn't starve. All I had were my books, but sometimes, the candle burned all the way down and I sat in darkness. And one day, they left. And I was alone. And that's when she came back."

The hairs on my arms stood on end as if the room had been electrified. My ears popped as a spectral form breached the door to the secret room. She wore a long dress, and her hair hung down against her shoulders. I pressed against the wall, trying to make myself invisible, but the woman was oblivious. The house was telling a story I wasn't part of. The Lady in White had returned.

As she crossed the room, her white glow illuminated the cowering figure in the corner. The disfigured boy had become a man. His clothes were ripped and tattered, and his skin was covered in dirt and grime.

His pale skin seemed almost translucent, and his hair grew in long, uneven patches.

"She read me stories every night, just like before."

The boy lay on the dirty wood floor and clutched at his stomach as he seemed to shrink in on himself. "Oh, I was so hungry, locked in that room, but she stayed with me until the end." A burst of light shot from his chest until I could see nothing but bright white.

I stood in the front yard of the house, staring up at it as if it were some mysterious monolith.

"And we were together. For years. For a century. She protected me from those who wanted to harm me. She told me stories every night. Until your friends came and took her away from me."

Brakes squeaked behind me as a nondescript white van with a blue stripe running down its side parked in the driveway.

"Once they took her bones, she couldn't stay, no matter how much I begged her to. And I was alone again."

As the car pulled away, I faced the house and looked up at the disfigured man in the window.

"Why did you make Owen kill himself?" My voice came as a whisper. I needed to confirm my suspicions.

"I had to," the voice replied. "It was the only way she would come. I tried with the other girl, but I scared her away."

"She will never be your mother," I said. "No matter how much you want her to be. Your mother's gone. I'm sorry, but she's gone. She's resting now."

The voice went infantile. "But I want her back. And if I can't have her, I'll have your friend. She will never leave here, and if you try to take her, she will cut you to pieces. It's only a matter of time before I can convince her to take the last step, and then she'll be mine forever. So leave us be, chickadee, and take the man with you while you still can. She is mine now."

I tried to piece together an escape plan. I didn't want to leave Amy behind, but the ghoul was right. She wouldn't go willingly, and forcing her to do so might have terrible consequences.

"We'll leave." My breath came in a puff that trailed toward the house. "I'll grab Tyler, and we'll drive away. You can have her." The words felt sour on my tongue.

"Very well," the voice replied.

A gust of wind picked up, and snow swirled around me. The storm roared in my ears, and darkness replaced the light.

"Where did you go?" I called out into the black.

An electric furnace burst to life, and I was once again in the basement. The large heap of coal and body lying atop it were both gone. I stepped toward the staircase and slowly climbed the stairs, keeping a vigilant eye on my surroundings.

The front door had been left open, and I sucked in the cool winter air as I stepped toward it. Freedom was so close. I could have gotten in my car and driven away. It could have been that simple. I filled my lungs once more then turned toward the staircase.

Tyler's pounding carried down the hallway. He must have still been hammering away at the door, not realizing how futile his efforts were.

As I walked the second-floor hallway, I eyed the jug of varnish and dirty polishing rags next to my bedroom door, just where I'd remembered them. I grabbed the jug and a rag then lunged inside.

The door slammed behind me, and the voice boomed from the walls. "What are you doing?"

Tyler spun around. "How the fuck did you get out here?"

"The dumbwaiter." I popped the cap off the varnish and stuck the rag inside. "I'm sorry for what happened to you, but this ends now." I locked eyes with Tyler. "Give me your lighter."

He frantically fished in his pocket and tossed the lighter in my direction.

I held the light to the end of the rag. "Let Amy go, or I light it."

Tyler's eyes widened. "What are you talking about?"

"And then you'll all die," the voice replied.

I flicked the flint wheel, and a spark flew from its edge. "And you'll lose your house. All your books. All your stories. You'll have nothing. So unlock the goddamned door or find out just how serious I am."

I reached for the knob to the secret room and twisted. The door latch clicked, and the door pulled free from the frame.

Tyler shook his head. "I guess I loosened it for you."

Amy sat in the rocking chair, cradling a small, swaddled bundle. When she heard us, she looked up and held her fingers to her lips. "Shh." Her eyes were wide and wild, underlined by deep bags, as if she hadn't slept for weeks. "The baby's sleeping."

The disfigured man stood watching, obscured by shadows.

"Amy, none of this is real. Owen is gone, and so is the baby."

Her eyes darted toward mine. "You're a liar!"

I stared at the silhouette of the man in the corner and held the lighter to the rag once more. "Look for yourself."

"Of course he's real." Amy lifted the edge of the blanket and peered inside. A look of horror crossed her face, and she let the bundle fall from her arms. The sheet fell away, and a misshapen human skull rolled free and stopped at my feet.

I searched the room for the rest of the skeleton and found it huddled in the far corner. I pointed. "See, it's the house that's doing this to you, Amy. A man died here. They locked him in this room, and he starved to death. It's terrible and tragic, but he's not your child. He's not Owen. He's just pretending."

Amy eyed the skull. She seemed to have snapped out of whatever hold the house had on her. "What's happening?" She rose from the chair and sidestepped the skull.

I turned toward Tyler. "Get her out of here. I'll be right behind you."

Tyler wrapped his arm around Amy's waist and led her through the doorway and down the hall. I followed close behind.

The house seemed to take the threat seriously, and as Amy and Tyler crossed the threshold into the yard, I turned to take one last look.

"Don't you want to stay with me, chickadee?" A voice came from behind. "It would be just like when you were a little girl."

I spun around, and my father stood between me and the door. "Stop with the games."

The floorboards creaked under my feet, and the house groaned around me.

"Don't you love me anymore, chickadee?" he asked.

His words took the air out of my lungs.

"We've been over this. You're not real," I said through gritted teeth. "And if you don't step out of my way, I will burn this house to the ground."

My father cocked his head to the side. "I'm the closest thing to your dad that you'll ever have again. I assure you, chickadee, if you walk away from this house, you walk away from me. You might see me in your dreams, but you'll never feel my touch or hear my voice again." His lip quivered.

"I will always love my father." I flicked the wheel of the lighter, igniting a small flame. "But my father is gone. And my memories are enough."

Dad's smile slipped into an uneven frown. His forehead bulged until it consumed one of his eyes, and he stumbled awkwardly to the side as if his legs had become uneven. I recognized the green of his iris, glowing from the light of the foyer chandelier.

I kept the jug close to the flame, holding it out toward him as I approached the front door. He stared at me, expression shifting between one of anger and longing.

Tyler shouted from his van. I wanted to run toward him, to run from this place as fast as I could.

When I stepped outside, I let go of the button that kept the lighter ignited. I tossed the can of varnish aside, and it hit the front porch, spilling deep-brown ooze into the fresh snow that had accumulated on the porch's edge.

"Don't leave me alone here." A wail came from behind. I didn't know what came over me, but I turned back toward the house and the disfigured man standing in the entryway. Pity radiated through my chest. I steadied myself on the first step and held my hand out. "Come outside."

The man wiped his eyes. "Just go."

"You don't have to stay here anymore," I insisted. "You can leave anytime you want. The door is open. Just step outside."

"I can't." His voice quivered.

"If you were trapped, you'd still be sitting in that room upstairs. You can leave if you want to."

The man's expression soured. "I can't!" he screamed. "Now, go away!"

A burst of hot air knocked me off the steps and into the snow.

Tyler rushed to my side and helped me up. "Let's get the hell out of here."

CHAPTER TWENTY-TWO

A For Sale sign swayed back and forth in front of the wrought iron gate. I'd asked Amy if I could visit the house one last time. The three of us hadn't been back since the night we'd escaped in the winter storm. Amy hadn't even come back to collect her belongings. Rather, she'd hired movers to box up all her stuff and deliver it to her new apartment on the opposite end of town.

The gate ground against its frame as I pushed it open, and I garnered a few odd looks from passersby. The story had made the paper, and although Amy had feared losing everything, she had buyers lining up before the house went on the market. At first, I was angry with her for pawning the place off on some unsuspecting victim, but that changed when the Lady in White came home to rest for good.

I walked around the side of the house to the back-yard, and dead leaves crunched under my feet. A small area had been fenced off around the old oak tree, and two new headstones stuck out of the earth. Amy had contacted the distant family of the Lady in White, and they'd agreed to release her remains to be buried on the property. The police had removed the disfig-ured skeleton from the secret room on the second floor, but eventually, her son came home too. I wondered if he'd moved on after he was properly buried. Despite the pain he'd caused, my heart still ached for him.

I looked up at the structure that had tormented so many of my dreams. The curtains fluttered in the second-floor window. The man of the house stared back at me. And he stood alone. I waved, not knowing how else to greet the ghoul who had nearly taken the lives of three of my friends. He rested his palm on the glass. He must not have found peace after all.

I pitied him, locked away in the darkness until adulthood came creeping in like a fleeting sliver of light under the doorway. *But what about his mother?*

I returned to the car and fished for my copy of *Grimm's Fairy Tales* sandwiched between cardboard boxes filled with new products for the New York Spookfest. One box held a mock-up for a new issue of *Urban Rot*, Tyler's magazine. He'd made good on his promise to collaborate, and I'd spent more time in Detroit since leaving Amy's.

The early autumn breeze was crisp against my skin. The scar on my arm still itched from time to time, but the doctors had done a hell of a job stitching me back together.

Amy had given me the code to the Realtor's lockbox, and I twisted the tiny numbered dials until the lock clicked. I slid the key into the lock and twisted, but as I clasped the door handle, the hairs on the back of my neck stood on end.

I saw her there, standing in the front yard, surrounded by a spectral white glow. The Lady in White lifted her hand to the man pressed against the window glass and beckoned.

He must come into the daylight. The thought flashed across my mind as if someone else had put it there. I let go of the lockbox. A tear trickled down my cheek as I ran my fingers over the book's embossed letters one final time then set it on the front porch. The door to the hidden room had been opened. The son's remains had been laid to rest, and he'd been placed next to the person he'd longed for most. But it wasn't enough to free him. No one could force him outside. If he wanted another story, he could step into the daylight and claim it for himself.

The firelight flickered off the creek's surface as we warmed ourselves by the campfire. I stuck a branch into the flame, then pulled it out a few moments later and traced my name with the glowing ember. Dad and I didn't go camping often. I was built for the indoors, air conditioning, and video games, so it took some convincing to get me to spend time in the unforgiving wilderness.

We talked of many things by the fire. Dad told stories of growing up—stories that he told with the same vigor even though they'd been told a dozen times before. We talked about superhero movies and what I'd been up to in school. Eventually, we moved to more abstract things, and somehow we landed on ghosts.

The man was stone-faced when it came to religion. He'd grown up Baptist but only went to church to watch me sing with the choir or perform God-awful interpretations of famous Bible stories as a part of the youth group. I was a budding atheist, and I think my outspokenness annoyed him sometimes, but I still do not know whether he believed in life after death or God at all. He kept that to himself.

That night we agreed that whoever died first would flip a light switch to let the other know they were ok. It was silly and a bit morbid, but the memory stuck with me.

I was at dad's side the day he died in 2019. For all the buildup and existential angst involved, death comes more as a whimper than a bang. Eventually, he just stopped. My sister and her kids were staying with him too, and we all just sort of stared at each other. What do we do now? It's a question that I still ask myself sometimes.

In a sick twist of irony, my estranged brother was working as a flower delivery driver and—this is too unbelievable to make up—delivered flowers to dad's funeral. It was a cruel way to find out his father had died.

Dad's death brought me closer to my brother and sister. I was the only child of my dad's second marriage, and my siblings were ten years older and never lived with me, so I grew up with only-child tendencies.

Shortly after dad's passing, my siblings and I were

standing in Dad's kitchen. My brother mentioned that he'd woken up at home in the middle of the night, and all the house lights had been turned on. I never shared dad's and my death pact with anyone and had forgotten about it until my brother told the story. The skeptic in me thinks that there's a logical explanation, but I wanted to believe it was dad.

My sister and I had spent a lot of time with dad during his illness. We didn't have closure so much as time, and time is the ultimate currency. My brother wasn't as lucky. Perhaps dad wanted to say one last goodbye. Perhaps he wanted my brother to know that he was at peace. Perhaps he wanted to apologize.

Dad had an old clock he'd purchased in Germany during his military service. It was a beautiful clock, but it had been broken for my entire life and hung in a sad state on the wall, with its pendulum laying in the clock's base like a severed appendage. Dad had always wanted to fix the clock but never got around to it. My sister took it after dad's death, and she stored it in her bedroom closet. One day, a strange noise from the closet scared the crap out of her. The clock chimed for the first time in several decades and swiftly broke again.

Dad had joked that he wanted to be stuffed and mounted when he died and put in the entryway so he could spook anyone who came inside. Creating Charlie was as close as I could get to granting his tongue-in-cheek final wish. He approached every serious issue with levity and a sly grin. "It is what it is" was his favorite phrase.

Although Charlie was, in many ways, an extreme departure from my dad, the grief felt for him was genuine. Robin's feelings were genuine because I felt them. Writing this book allowed me to confront my darkest fears and emotions. The opportunity to explore and make peace with the darkness is what makes Horror so powerful, and telling this story has been my first true attempt to be honest about the experience. I had withheld my grief like an illness, as if others might catch the darkness if they got too close. I'm thankful for Robin, who allowed me to address my thoughts and feelings honestly. And, if you've read this far, I'm thankful that you came along for the ride.

At times, it's hard to avoid nihilism. What is this all for? Why are we here? After countless sleepless nights, I've settled on this—we may occupy but a small slice in time, but the impact of our relationships spiderwebs through the universe and persists long after we're gone. We've probably changed people's lives without even realizing it. Somewhere, someone needs us. Someone needs our support, our friendship, our love, and our story. And, maybe, someone is waiting for us to leave the light on.

ABOUT THE AUTHOR

Chris Cooper is a writer, college professor, novice coffee roaster, and recovering engineer. He lived and worked in Japan, where he developed an obscure obsession for fancy fountain pens and currently lives in Ohio with his partner and Australian Cattle Terrier. Both enjoy long walks. Chris writes horror and supernatural thrillers full of colorful three-dimensional characters, macabre adventures, and twisty turny plots.